Murder On Tour

V. M. BURNS

Kensington Publishing Corp.
www.kensingtonbooks.com

KENSINGTON BOOKS are published by

Kensington Publishing Corp.
119 West 40th Street
New York, NY 10018

Special book excerpts or customized printings can also be created to fit specific needs. For details, write or phone the office of the Kensington Sales Manager: Kensington Publishing Corp., 119 West 40th Street, New York, NY 10018. Attn. Sales Department. Phone: 1-800-221-2647.

The K and Teapot logo is a trademark of Kensington Publishing Corp.

ISBN: 978-1-4967-3949-0 (ebook)

ISBN: 978-1-4967-3948-3

First Kensington Trade Paperback Printing: December 2023

10 9 8 7 6 5 4 3 2 1

Printed in the United States of America

Books by Valerie Burns

Baker Street Mysteries
TWO PARTS SUGAR, ONE PART MURDER
MURDER IS A PIECE OF CAKE

Books by Valerie Burns writing as V. M. Burns

Mystery Bookshop Mysteries
THE PLOT IS MURDER
READ HERRING HUNT
THE NOVEL ART OF MURDER
WED, READ & DEAD
BOOKMARKED FOR MURDER
A TOURIST'S GUIDE TO MURDER
KILLER WORDS
BOOKCLUBBED TO DEATH
MURDER ON TOUR

Dog Club Mysteries
IN THE DOG HOUSE
THE PUPPY WHO KNEW TOO MUCH
BARK IF IT'S MURDER
PAW AND ORDER
SIT, STAY, SLAY

Published by Kensington Publishing Corp.

Murder On Tour

Chapter 1

"You look like you could use a stiff drink."

My grandmother grabbed me by the arm and hoisted me up from the table where I sat with a smile frozen on my face, trying to make eye contact with people who were doggedly determined *not* to make eye contact with me.

"Nana Jo, what are you doing here? Aren't you supposed to be running the bookstore?" I asked although, even to my own ears, I recognized the relief in my voice.

Nana Jo waved away my objections. "Dawson has everything well in hand."

"I know Dawson's capable of running the bookstore, but I thought he had football practice?"

My assistant and head baker for my mystery bookstore was also the quarterback for the MISU Tigers football team, so his free time was limited.

"The twins are in town for the weekend," Nana Jo said, "and they agreed to help out so I could come to see you on your panel this afternoon."

She said *panel* as though I was about to present before Congress. I hated to destroy her illusions. "Nana Jo, it's just going to be four authors sitting on a stage answering questions. Based on the panels I sat through this morning, there may only be two or three people in the audience."

"Doesn't matter. I don't care if you're reading your book in a telephone booth, I am here to support you. Do you really think I'd miss seeing my favorite granddaughter at the North Harbor Book Festival?"

I smiled at my grandmother's use of the term *favorite*. When she was talking to me, I was her favorite, and when she was talking to my sister, Jenna, she was her favorite. Still, it made me smile. "Not much to see. At least, not here."

Michigan Southwestern University, or Miss You, as the locals referred to it, was well known for hosting a prestigious book festival on campus every year. Award-winning, critically acclaimed authors from around the world converged on the small town of North Harbor, Michigan, each year. This year was no different. The halls of the Hechtman-Ayers Performing Arts Center were teeming with tweed-suited writers with unlit pipes clenched between their teeth, academic-looking women dressed in business suits with sensible shoes who were referred to by renowned critics as *literary geniuses*, and me, an unknown, first-time cozy mystery author, who was way out of her league amongst so many renowned authors.

The main hallway in the industrial-styled arts building was lined with folding tables covered in black tablecloths. At various times of the day, fans could purchase their favorite author's books from a classroom turned into a makeshift bookstore. They bought the book and took it to the author's table for signing. All of the tables were identical, except for the folded name tent that identified which author sat where. Some authors included an additional sheet of paper with a schedule that indicated when they would be manning their tables.

The main hallway was a hive of activity with tables lining both sides. At the end of the hallway and around the corner was one final table. Strategically placed between the men's restroom and the fire escape, and hidden behind a large fake palm tree, was my table.

Nana Jo looked around. "Why are you here in the cheap seats?"

"I was only added at the last minute when one of the other authors canceled. So . . ." I shrugged. "Besides, I don't really write the type of books that these other authors write."

"Well, you're right there," Nana Jo said. "Your books sell. People actually read your books."

"I mean most of these authors write weightier, more important things. They write literary fiction, biographies, and books that are . . . deep." I sighed. "I write British historical cozy mysteries . . . escapist fiction."

"Pshaw! You don't believe that drivel." Nana Jo was five feet ten and close to two hundred pounds. When she looked down her nose at me, I felt even smaller than my five feet four inches.

"Well . . ."

"That's a lot of horse pucky, and you know it. Samantha Marie Washington, you're an intelligent woman, and you not only own one of the most successful independent bookstores in the area, you've written a great mystery with an engaging plot and interesting characters."

I chuckled. "I own the only bookstore in the area. Independent or otherwise."

"Piffle. Details. Details. Details."

"You know what I mean. My book is . . . entertaining, but being here made me realize that my book isn't going to change the world. No one is going to read my book and start a movement that will stop human trafficking, reduce the effects of global warming, or save the Amur leopard from extinction. Did you know there are estimated to be less than one hundred of those wild leopards left in Russia and China?"

"That's terrible, but what does that have to do with the price of tea in North Harbor, Michigan?"

"Those were the people I met this morning at the author breakfast. There we were. The four of us all talking about our books. The author of a book that exposes human trafficking, a book on global warming, a woman who spent five years in the Russian wilderness photographing the Amur leopard, and me with my escapist cozy mystery."

Nana Jo lifted my chin and gazed in my eyes. "Those are all noble causes, and I hope those books will be successful and achieve everything they were intended to achieve. But don't discount the importance of escapist fiction. Books are subjective, and people read books for different reasons. Given everything that's happened in the world, many of us need to escape to maintain our sanity. Before your granddad died, I spent two weeks in the hospital . . . waiting. I sat in that hospital room and read Nora Roberts as if it held the keys to life and death. I was obsessed."

"I remember."

She shook her head. "I'm sure those books were the only things that kept me from falling to pieces. So, don't you go knocking escapist fiction."

I hugged my grandmother. "Thanks. I needed that reminder."

After a few moments, Nana Jo pulled away, sniffed, and dabbed at her eyes with a tissue. "Now, it's lunchtime. Let's blow this mortuary and grab some grub."

My panel discussion was less than one hour away, so I didn't want to venture too far from the auditorium. In fact, I wanted to be early to give myself time to collect my thoughts. Frank Patterson, my fiancé, taught me how to do a technique he called tactical breathing. He suggested that I sit in a quiet room for fifteen minutes before the panel and take slow, deep breaths to help steady my nerves before the panel. Frank used to do top-secret stuff in the military before he retired and moved to North Harbor to pursue his dream of opening a restaurant. He swears that tactical breathing will help me stay calm. I was doubtful but willing to try anything.

We decided to keep it simple and went to the Gridiron, the restaurant inside the student union. Normally, I loved nothing better than a greasy Gridiron burger with cheddar cheese and an order of extra crispy onion rings, but my nerves went into hyperdrive. My throat contracted, and my stomach turned into a cement mixer. Any crumbs that made it to my stomach were immediately tossed, turned, and tumbled around until eventually hardening into what felt like rocks. After just a few bites, I gave up trying.

"I don't know why you're so nervous," Nana Jo said. "You used to teach English to high school teenagers."

"Not the same thing. I knew what I was talking about."

"No one knows mysteries like you do. You own a mystery bookstore, for God's sake." Nana Jo reached for my onion rings. "Are you going to eat those?"

I shook my head and slid the greasy rings across to her tray. "I know mysteries, but this is my first published book. I mean, what if they ask me some question that I can't answer? What if I start babbling and make a fool of myself?"

"I've never heard you babble, and you will not make a fool of yourself. Besides, it's only one hour. What could possibly go wrong?"

"Famous last words."

I hurried back to the Hechtman-Ayer auditorium, with thirty minutes to practice my breathing. Jillian Clark was the daughter of one of Nana Jo's friends and my assistant Dawson's girlfriend. She'd performed many times on this stage, and she told me about a small room backstage that would be the perfect place to relax and practice breathing. It was just off to the side of what she called the "green room," where performers relaxed when not on stage. I found the right door, flipped the light switch, and went inside.

Jillian was right. This room was perfect. It was a small closet, but it was quiet.

I turned off the light. I shook my arms and legs and stretched. Then, when I closed my eyes, I inhaled for four counts. Held for four counts. Exhaled for six counts. Held for two. When I was done, I did it again. And again. Rinse and repeat. I don't know how many times I went through the exercise, but after a few minutes, I could feel myself calm down. Maybe there was something to this breathing stuff after all. I was just about to go through the exercise again when a door slammed, and my calm was broken.

"Judith."

"Hello, Nora."

Holy cow. Nora must be Nora Cooper, and Judith must be featured presenter Judith Hunter. The other panelists are here, and I'm trapped in a closet.

"You've got a lot of nerve coming here. I can't believe you had the guts to show your face in public after what you did."

"Actually, it didn't take any nerve at all. I'm the featured guest. But then you always were overly dramatic, Nora."

"Overly dramatic?"

"Yes. Overly dramatic. Just like your books, full of outrageous dialogue, over-the-top characters, and ridiculous plots that couldn't possibly happen. That's so like you."

Ouch.

"I heard you were going to be here, but I was surprised when I learned they were including you in the panel discussion. I didn't think they'd lower themselves to including self-published authors at the North Harbor Book Festival."

That's not very nice.

"Actually, the correct term is *indie published*," Nora said, "and the Festival Committee must have been looking for authors who actually write books that sell."

"I know. My latest book is on all of the major bestseller lists."

"Your book? If you weren't so pathetic, you'd be funny. You mean my book. The book you stole from me."

What?

"Watch it," Judith said. "If you say that to anyone else, my attorney assures me that we'll sue you for every dime you have left."

Nora laughed. It was a bit hysterical, but there was something else in that laugh—the slightest bit triumphant.

"What's so funny?" Judith asked.

"Worried? You should be. You thought there would be no way I could prove that you stole my manuscript. But, it turns out, you're wrong. I wrote *The Corpse Danced at Midnight*, and I can prove it. Not only am I going to prove that you're a thief and a liar, but I'm going to make sure that you're humiliated and made a laughingstock. You won't be able to show your face in public. When I get done with you—"

"Well, well, well."

"Scarlet, what are you doing here?" Judith huffed. "What is this, old home week?"

"Sounds like another member of the I-Hate-Judith-Hunter Fan Club. Hi, I'm Scarlet MacDunkin."

"Nora Cooper. Pleased to meet you, but I'm not just a member of the club. I'm the founder and president."

"Then let me shake your hand." Scarlet laughed. Unlike

Nora's triumphant, slightly deranged laugh, Scarlet's was husky and dripping with cynicism.

"Gawd, Clark. What have you gotten me into?"

"Judith, I'm so sorry, but I thought it might be best if we could just all get together and talk things through, then maybe we could avoid an expensive and embarrassing court case. Coming to this event and being on the panel with you were Nora's conditions. I didn't know Scarlet would be here."

Who is this man?

"Oh, when I heard Nora was coming, fire-breathing dragons couldn't have kept me away," Scarlet said.

"And the fourth person on the panel, Samantha Washington, is she part of the conspiracy to destroy me too?" Judith said with an edge in her voice.

Me? Heck, I don't even know any of these people.

"No, actually, she's nobody, a last-minute replacement," Clark said. "Michelle Ackerman backed out. Samantha Washington is just some local who's written her first book. A British historical cozy. The organizers thought a local might attract the hometown crowd. Plus, she's cheap. They didn't have to pay for travel or lodging."

Cheap? Well, I guess that explains it. I wasn't invited here because my book is selling well or because any of the organizers liked my book. I was invited because I'm cheap.

"Well, I'm not going on stage with both of these barracudas and a rookie," Judith said, "so you can just figure out another plan."

"Judith, you signed a contract," Clark said.

Scarlet laughed.

"Scared?" Nora said. "You should be. When I get finished with you, you're going to wish you'd never even thought about messing with me."

The threat sounds serious. I gasped and took a step backward. Unfortunately, the closet wasn't big enough for sudden movements, and I hit my head on the back wall of the closet.

"What's that?"

Crap.

The door was wrenched open.

"Who are you?" a pasty-faced man asked.

"Me? I'm nobody. I'm just the cheap, local author reporting for duty."

Chapter 2

Getting caught eavesdropping is never good. My first instinct was to tuck my tail between my legs and crawl out of the room. I stared from one set of eyes to the others. It wasn't just my imagination that I saw contempt, pity, and scorn reflected back toward me. In a split second, I had an inspiration.

What Would Nana Jo Do?

"Finally! I thought I'd never get out of that closet." I shoved past the group into the room.

I didn't know any of the authors personally. Their pictures were in the program book, but owning a bookshop meant that I not only knew who they were, but I'd read at least one of each of their books.

Judith Hunter raised a perfectly arched brow. "So, you're saying you were locked in the closet that entire time?"

Judith was tall and thin, with thick blond hair and icy blue eyes. One look told me she was a runner, and on behalf of short, plump women everywhere, I felt an instant hatred of her lean figure. She was an attractive woman, and she knew it. Her lips were thin, and there was something hard in her eyes. Of course, she'd just been ganged up on by two women and found a third listening, so I gave her a pass on the stink eye. Before her breakout novel, *The Corpse Danced at Midnight*, she wrote doggedly boring police procedurals and true crime. Her latest novel had been a refreshing departure from her normal writing style and was filled with humor, emotion, and a surprising plot twist at the end. Critics called it brilliant, and it released atop not only the *New York Times* Best Sellers list but also every other list in the U.S. and abroad. In fact, it was rumored that the film rights were sold for an astounding nine-figure deal.

"Funny, we didn't hear you knocking or yelling to get out." Judith tilted her head to the side and glared. "Are you sure you don't want to revise that story?"

"Why should I? That's my story, and I'm sticking to it." I flopped down on the sofa.

"Ha!" Nora Cooper snorted. "I think I like the new kid on the block."

Nora was shorter than me, which probably put her at five feet two. She might have been thin once, but that ship had sailed. Her clothes might have fit nicely once too, but today they seemed to be at least two sizes too small. She had thick curly red hair. Not auburn. Red. Between her pasty white skin and curly red hair, she bore a striking resemblance to Ronald McDonald, minus the cheerful smile and big clown shoes. Her feet were small. The book that I'd read was one of her early books. If I had to categorize it, I'd call it romantic suspense. Nana Jo called it erotic suspense. Heavy on the romance and light on the suspense.

Scarlet flashed a fake smile. "Ah, you write those cute cozy mysteries, right?"

Scarlet MacDunkin went by Mac to her friends. I wasn't a friend, and I wouldn't be calling her Mac.

Cute cozy mysteries indeed.

She had brown eyes and mousy brown hair that she wore

in a style common in the 1980s. Apart from the 1980s hair, she was of average height. Average weight. And above-average intelligence. Scarlet wrote dark domestic suspense filled with such graphic descriptions of evil that even Nana Jo needed to burn sage to clear the negative energy and spend a month reading humorous cozies to get her mind in a good place after reading just one of Scarlet's dark, twisted tales. The truly scary thing was that she always smiled and spoke like a kindergarten teacher, even in a TikTok video while reading one of the most graphically violent scenes in her book.

"That's just so adorable. Sometimes, I need a break from all of the serious crime fiction, and I like to read a cozy mystery. They are always so light and funny with dogs and food." Scarlet leaned close as though whispering a secret to a friend. "I've even watched an episode or two of *Murder, She Wrote*."

Serious mysteries? Change of plans. Time to switch from What Would Nana Jo Do. Nana Jo would shove her foot up Scarlet's—

"Shut up, Scarlet," Judith said. "I'm not in the mood for your condescending passive-aggressive nonsense today." She paced from one end of the room to the other.

The volcano wave of burning lava that crept up Scarlet's neck and the quick flash of lightning in her eyes were the only signs of irritation she showed. Quickly, both were squashed, and she gave a loud obnoxious cackle and plastered her phony smile back in place.

"Mrs. Washington, I'm Clark Cunningham, and I'm terribly sorry for . . . everything. What a terrible experience. I will report the faulty lock to the organizers, and I hope you will forgive me for any negative comments made in the heat of the moment."

Not likely.

Nana Jo would have described Clark Cunningham as someone who had been "rode hard and put away wet." His blue eyes were cloudy and darted around the room quickly like a scared rabbit. His skin was pockmarked from bouts of acne and had a yellow tinge that made me question the state of his liver. His gray hair was thin and hung lifelessly on his scalp. I didn't need to get close to know he'd smell like alcohol. His suit was wrinkled and hung off his frame.

Despite his appearance, there was something in Cunningham's demeanor that made me want to be kind to him. "Thank you, Mr. Cunningham."

Scarlet MacDunkin snorted.

The door opened, and in waltzed Dr. Leonard Peters. Dr. Peters was a lawyer and professor of criminal justice at MISU and somewhat of a local celebrity. In addition to his scholarly work, he was a legal consultant who often appeared on the news. Physically fit and distinguished, with silver hair and a winning smile, Dr. Peters had been commandeered to facilitate the panel.

"Hello, authors. I'm Dr. Peters, but please call me Leonard. I'm going to be facilitating what I hope will be a lively discussion about crime fiction and wanted to find out if there's anything that I can do to make the panel run more smoothly." Dr. Peters smiled broadly.

Judith Hunter pointed at Nora Cooper. "Yeah, you can remove her."

To say Dr. Peters appeared shocked would have been the understatement of the century.

He looked from Judith to Nora and then around to the rest of us, as if looking for someone to explain the punch line of the joke to him. "Excuse me?"

"You heard me. I refuse to go on stage and appear on any panels with that woman. So, you can make a decision here and now. It's either her or me!" Judith folded her arms across her chest and stared.

Dr. Peters sputtered, "Well . . . I don't know . . . I don't . . ."

Clark Cunningham stepped up. "Nora, perhaps it would be better if we—"

"Oh, no you don't!" Nora screamed. "Don't you dare take her side, again. I have as much of a right to be here as her—more, since I wrote *The Corpse Danced at Midnight*, the book she's taking credit for. That's my book! The book she's so proud of and that got her invited here as the star is my book!"

The door was flung open, and a small woman with bright teal glasses marched inside. "What's going on in here? We can hear you screeching like cats in heat throughout the auditorium."

Nora wailed.

Dr. Peters hurried over to the woman and quickly whispered in her ear. "Mrs. Graves. It appears we have a bit of a problem."

Mrs. Graves was a woman of decision. She turned to a lanky male student, who trailed her like a shadow, and whispered a few words. The student left and within a minute returned with a pimply faced security guard.

"Please escort Miss Cooper to my office," Mrs. Graves ordered.

Nora wailed even louder.

The security guard might have appeared young, but between him and Clark Cunningham, they managed to propel Nora Cooper out of the room.

Nora didn't leave quietly. Instead, she screamed, "Thief! I'll get you for this, Judith. Just you wait. You won't get away with this."

The threats decreased to a dull rumble and eventually ended completely.

I glanced at Judith Hunter, who let a smug look slip through her mask before it was quickly removed. "Thank you, Mrs. Graves. Clearly, you could see that the woman is deranged. I just couldn't go on stage with her. She's a loose cannon."

Whatever Mrs. Graves saw, she kept it to herself. Instead, she turned to Dr. Peters. "Is there anything else you need?"

Dr. Peters gave a quick glance around the room. Seeing no further problems, he shook his head.

"Great. Then we should be back on track." She turned and left, followed by her assistant.

I longed to get up and follow Mrs. Graves out of the room too, but I didn't. Instead, I sat perfectly still like a deer caught in headlights. Perhaps if I didn't move, I could become invisible. They might forget that I was even there, and I wouldn't have to go on stage at all.

"Now that that's all settled," Dr. Peters said, "I'll make a brief announcement that Ms. Cooper was suddenly taken ill, and adjust my questions. I'm sure we can have an insightful discussion among the three of you." He looked at each of us. "As they say in show business, let's break a leg."

Based on Nora Cooper's threats, I hoped a leg would be the only thing broken.

Chapter 3

I could have saved myself a ton of stress if I'd known that the panel discussion wasn't about me. I should have known it wasn't about me. I was a debut novelist. A *cozy* debut novelist who was only invited at the last minute because I was local and cheap. Judith Hunter was the guest of honor for the book festival and the main attraction. Scarlet MacDunkin and I were the backdrops against which the festival organizers presented their star. We served the same purpose as the velvet fabric used to set off sparkling diamonds in a jewelry store window or the *You might also like* books that I strategically placed behind bestsellers in my bookshop displays. My British historical cozy mystery and Scarlet's grisly tales of suspense were in contrast to Judith Hunter's "twisty, intriguing story with emotionally flawed but compelling characters." At least, that's what Dr. Peters said while introducing Judith. About me, he mentioned that *Murder at Wickfield Lodge* was my debut novel and that I must be awed sitting on stage next to an international bestselling author.

Yeah, sure.

Scarlet MacDunkin knew her role. She was the side dish,

not the entrée. However, just like the sour-cream smashed potatoes with fried shallots that Frank served with his perfectly prepared prime rib, Scarlet made the most of her moment in the spotlight. She smiled broadly, joked, and complimented Judith with wild abandon. At least, that's the way it appeared. However, only someone who'd spent time in a closet listening to a private conversation would understand that every compliment was a backhanded slap and each accolade a sharp jab to the solar plexus. I knew, and a vein throbbing on the side of Judith's head told me that she knew as well.

"Judith's writing shows such maturity. It leaps from the page like poetry. Was it T. S. Eliot who said, 'Immature poets imitate; mature poets steal; bad poets deface what they take, and good poets make it into something better, or at least something different.'"

Judith gritted her teeth and smiled, although it seemed more like a grimace. "Scarlet, you are too kind, but I'm just a babe when it comes to writing. You've been doing this for decades longer than me."

Ouch.

For nearly one hour, Judith and Scarlet lobbed thinly veiled insults at each other like tennis balls at Wimbledon. Dr. Peters tossed an occasional question my way to keep the conversation balanced, but I wasn't playing their game, and I was thankful to be left out and watch from the sidelines.

Afterward, we headed to our tables to sign books. As the guest of honor, Judith's table was just outside the auditorium. Not surprisingly, a crowd had gathered to get their books signed, and Clark Cunningham and Mrs. Graves's student were herding the enthusiastic guests into lines that wouldn't block the hall and pose a fire hazard.

En route to my table, I passed Scarlet MacDunkin's table, where a couple of students posed for selfies.

Down the hall and around the corner, I was shocked to

see a small crowd of people who erupted into a loud cheer. Nana Jo, several of her friends from Shady Acres Retirement Village, my sister Jenna Rutherford, and a few familiar faces from MISU and the community crowded my table.

I gazed at the familiar faces that had come out to show their support, and my gaze landed on Nana Jo's friends from Shady Acres Retirement Village.

"Where did all of you come from?" I asked.

Ruby Mae hugged me. "Josephine said you were nervous." Out of all of my grandmother's friends, she was my favorite. Ruby Mae Stevenson was a Black woman in her mid-sixties. Born in Alabama, Ruby Mae had lived in the north for close to half a century, but she never lost her Southern drawl.

"She sent your handsome fiancé to pick us up," Irma said. She hugged me and whispered in my ear, "If I were a few years younger, I might give you a run for your money."

Irma Starczewski was in her mid-eighties and the oldest of Nana Jo's friends. Barely five feet tall and one hundred pounds, Irma was what Nana Jo called a nymphomaniac.

"Josephine said you needed backup, so here we are," Dorothy Clark said. At six feet and close to three hundred pounds, Dorothy was a martial arts expert with a black belt in aikido. She was the closest to Nana Jo. "Now, who do you need me to take out?" Dorothy laughed.

My sister, Jenna Rutherford, sidled up next to me and whispered, "She's not joking. Your grandmother fired off a bazillion text messages ordering us to get here or else."

Jenna was older than me, but at five four, we were the same height and close to the same weight, although I tended to have about fifteen extra pounds.

"I'm surprised you came," I joked.

"She said she might need a lawyer to bail her out of jail if things got too rowdy."

"You're joking?"

Jenna shook her head. "No, and then she told me she was bringing her Peacemaker along just in case."

I looked around the crowd until I saw my grandmother's head pop up. "You don't think she meant it, do you?"

Jenna gave me a look that said, *You must be joking.*

"You're right. She wasn't joking."

Fortunately, my grandmother was an excellent shot, but that wasn't important at the moment.

My fiancé, Frank Patterson, came up holding a large bouquet of red roses. "Hello, beautiful." Frank leaned close and kissed me. He was five ten with soft brown eyes, salt-and-pepper hair, and a beard.

I inhaled. He always smelled of bacon, coffee, and Irish soap.

I pointed at the flowers. "Are those for me?"

"Yes, and if you're a good girl, I will make you a BLT minus the T." Frank owned a restaurant and loved to cook. Food was his love language, and he knew the way to my heart.

I gazed in his eyes and wondered for the millionth time how I had gotten so lucky. After the love of my life, my late husband, Leon, died, I never dreamed that I would ever fall in love again. How could there ever be anyone to replace the man I'd loved and shared my life with for seventeen years. Frank never tried to replace Leon. He merely found his own spot in my heart and took up residence.

"Alright, enough of the goo-goo eyes," Nana Jo said, taking the flowers. "Let's put these on your table and get this party started."

"Party?" I asked.

"Sure. You already had a book signing when your book first came out. So, we're here to show our love and support. Dawson's running the bookstore, but he wanted to show his support, so he made cupcakes." Nana Jo reached into a large bag and pulled out a plastic container filled with what looked like a sheet cake.

"Dawson made me a cake?"

"A cupcake cake." Nana Jo placed the container on the table and carefully lifted the cake out of the container.

It wasn't until the cake was on the table and viewed from the side that you could see that he had taken cupcakes and covered the top with frosting to make them look like a sheet cake. However, he had not only covered the cupcakes with frosting, but he had somehow had the image of my book cover imprinted on the frosting.

Dawson loved two things: football and baking. When he wasn't playing football for the MISU Tigers or taking classes, he worked and baked at the bookstore.

"It's beautiful," I said. "How did he do that?"

"Modern technology is wonderful," Nana Jo said. "Frank helped me get the special printer with edible ink and icing sheets."

Frank smiled. "It's an investment. Maybe Dawson can teach me to use it for the restaurant."

I reached up and kissed him again. "Thank you."

I gave my grandmother a hug. "I love you."

In addition to the cupcakes, Nana Jo had brought small cartons of water that looked like the milk cartons we used to get in elementary school. We put out the water, napkins, and paper plates, and everyone enjoyed the cupcakes, took pictures, and mingled.

After about thirty minutes, Jenna came over to where I was standing and talking to a couple of complete strangers who had attended the panel discussion and came to tell me they wanted to read my book. I spent enough time around college students to know that they simply wanted a cupcake, but I appreciated the subterfuge.

"I'm supposed to be in court in thirty minutes, so I have to go," Jenna said.

"Thanks for coming."

In a surprisingly un-Jenna-like manner, she hugged me and said, "I'm proud of you, Schleprock."

Schleprock. It had been years since she'd called me that. Schleprock was a gloomy and accident-prone character on the *Pebbles and Bamm-Bamm Show* cartoon that we watched when we were kids. Whenever I fell and skinned my knee or broke a limb, my sister would tease me by calling me "Bad Luck Schleprock." Over time, she'd shortened it to either Schleprock or Schlep. Thirty years ago, I hated the moniker, which I viewed as an insult. Over the decades, I didn't mind it as much.

Not long afterward, Frank got a call about a problem at the restaurant and had to leave too. Although, he promised he'd be by to pick me up on time for our date. He was my escort for the author awards banquet tonight.

A quick glance at my watch told me that I'd better pack up soon so I could run home and shower and change into the fancy dress I bought for the banquet. Thankfully, this was a weekend event, and soon it would be over and I could return where I belonged. For more years than I can remember, I dreamed about being a published author and traveling the world like Jessica Fletcher from *Murder, She Wrote*. I hoped to skip the whole find-a-dead-body-everywhere-I-went part. I just wanted to write books and mingle among other writers. Now, here I was. I was a published author. This was the last event on my first book tour. I had traveled to bookstores, libraries, and mini-cons in just a few short months. Yet, as I looked around at the established authors, I felt like an outsider. I couldn't wait until I was back on familiar turf. I longed for my bookstore, my poodles, and my obscure life. I didn't belong here.

We packed up the leftovers and headed out. I drove the girls back to Shady Acres and thanked them for coming out to support me. It meant a lot. These women didn't know a lot about mysteries, but they would defend me to the death if anyone said an unkind word about my book. Some days, you need people like that in your corner.

"I had a great time," Ruby Mae said. "My cousin's grandson works in the MISU library. It was nice to get a chance to talk to him."

Ruby Mae had a large family and even larger extended family network. Wherever we went, she always met family members or friends. On the rare instances when no family members were present, strangers would sit down and start talking to her. She had one of those faces that people felt they could talk to. And they did. People talked to Ruby Mae. Complete strangers shared their darkest secrets with her. That came in handy when we found ourselves needing information when sleuthing.

Back at the bookstore, I thanked Dawson for the wonderful cupcake cake.

Dawson was tall and thin, although not as thin as he'd been when he was in my high school English class. His coaches at the university wanted him to "bulk up." With the help of coaches, trainers, a calorie-intensive diet, and lots of strength training, he had gained twenty pounds of muscle. Although, his blush showed that he still hadn't learned how to accept compliments. Nana Jo was teaching him to accept compliments and store them up for the times when he found himself needing a boost after a negative article or a loss on the field. Maybe I needed to sit in on those lessons too.

"Don't you have practice?" Nana Jo said.

Dawson checked his watch. "Oh, man. If I'm late, Coach will make me run laps." He kissed both Nana Jo and me on the cheek and hurried out the back door. Dawson had stayed

in an apartment over my garage ever since his freshman year
of college when his father got drunk and beat him to a pulp.
Dawson found his way to my bookstore seeking sanctuary. In
him, I'd found someone who was like the son Leon and I had
never had. It might not have been a normal relationship between a shop owner and her assistant, but it worked for us.

There were just a few customers in the bookstore, so
Nana Jo and I sat down at one of the small bistro tables at the
back of the store and grabbed a cupcake and a cup of tea from
the counter.

I held the warm cup and inhaled the nutty aroma. Surrounded by books and with my two chocolate toy poodles,
Snickers and Oreo, curled up on my feet, I was in my happy
place. Here, no international bestselling authors talked down
to me. No one made me feel insignificant. No one called my
book "cute."

"So what was all that shouting about before the panel?"
Nana Jo asked.

"You heard that?"

"The whole campus heard it. That woman was shrieking
like a barn owl."

I took a few minutes and explained what happened in the
green room and how Nora Cooper had been forcibly removed.

"Any truth to the accusations?" Nana Jo asked.

I shrugged. "I suppose if it makes it to court, we'll find out."

"Humph," Nana Jo huffed.

We sat in companionable silence for a few moments.

"Are you going to tell me what's really wrong?" Nana Jo
gazed over her coffee cup at me.

"I don't know what you mean."

"Okay, but I know what's wrong with you. You have imposter syndrome. I heard a podcast on it." She swiped her
phone. "I'm sending you a link."

"A link to what?"

"To the podcast. Haven't you been listening? This woman is a therapist. She makes a lot of sense. I think you should listen to her. It might help you while you're interacting with those hoity-toity literary snobs."

My phone dinged, indicating that the podcast link had been delivered to my phone.

A customer approached the counter, and I stood to go check.

"Let me take care of this," Nana Jo said. "You go upstairs and get ready for your banquet." She moved to the front of the store.

I sat and tried to digest what just happened. My grandmother thinks I need a therapist. Great. I checked my phone. I had plenty of time to get ready. Actually, after the excitement we'd had today, I wasn't even sure I wanted to go. I would much rather stay home and cuddle with Snickers, Oreo, and Frank, or read a good book. But I didn't want to disappoint my publisher. My publicist, Larissa Addo, had worked hard arranging book readings, signings, Zoom meetings with booksellers, and even appearances at book clubs. My first book tour had been a success, thanks to Larissa. This was the last stop on the tour and the last thing I wanted was to disappoint her. The least I could do was to show up. Besides, if I didn't go, then Nana Jo would just feel she was right and I really did have imposter syndrome.

I forced myself up, dislodging the poodles, who were curled up on my feet, and headed to my office. I'd replaced an old garage door with a glass door when I bought the building. That door led outside to a small courtyard. I let Snickers and Oreo out to take care of business. Then, I went upstairs to my apartment.

When my late husband, Leon, and I talked about buying this building, we planned the upstairs as a rental. However, before Leon's death, he encouraged me to sell our house and move in instead. Not having to worry about selling enough books to cover the mortgage on the bookstore plus a house payment would eliminate the pressure I felt at quitting my steady job as a high school English teacher to open a bookstore. Plus, he knew me well enough to know that I would need the change in order to move on with my life. He was right.

The space was large, with more than two thousand square feet. It was open, with beautiful oak floors, brick walls with seventeen-foot ceilings, and windows stretching from floor to ceiling. Before moving in, I'd renovated the space to include a nice kitchen, two bedrooms, and two bathrooms. Several days each week, Nana Jo stayed with me in the spare bedroom and helped out at the bookstore. The rest of the time, she stayed in her house at Shady Acres Retirement Village.

Upstairs, the kitchen smelled like vanilla and sugar. The kitchen in Dawson's studio was tiny, so whenever he wanted to do serious baking, he came upstairs and baked from here. I wasn't complaining. I loved the heavenly smell of freshly baked cookies, brownies, whatever. I loved it even more because I wasn't the one baking them. This was home. My safe place. Yet, tonight the warm smells didn't calm my spirit. Instead, I felt antsy. I paced across the hardwood floors and tried to shake off the dark cloud that had settled in my gut from the moment the closet door opened. No, that wasn't true. If I were honest with myself, my gut had started shaking long before then. *When did it start?*

I paced, followed by Oreo. Snickers lay down on the rug in front of the sofa and watched. Oreo, the younger of the two poodles, hadn't grown jaded like his older sister. He dutifully trailed my steps in the hopes that it would lead somewhere—to a treat if nowhere else.

I needed to clear my mind. No tactical breathing. I knew

what I needed to do. I made another cup of tea, grabbed my laptop, and perched on a barstool. Before long, I glanced at the manuscript that I'd been working on earlier. It would be a sequel to *Murder at Wickfield Lodge*. Soon, I was lost in the British countryside.

⁓

Wickfield Lodge, English Country Home of Lord William Marsh: 1939

Lady Elizabeth Marsh loved the drawing room at Wickfield Lodge, the country estate that had been her husband's ancestral home. The room was large but comfortably furnished. A massive fireplace crackled as brightly colored flames filled the room with a soft glow and the aroma of earth, leaves, and a slightly sweet, nutty smell. Lady Elizabeth sat at the end of the sofa with a pile of yarn on her lap, busily knitting a fluffy baby blanket. She smiled at the thought that in a few short months, she would hold a new addition to the Marsh clan when her niece, Lady Daphne, and her husband, Lord James Browning, the 15th Duke of Kingfordshire, welcomed their new addition. Lady Elizabeth and her husband never had children of their own, but when her husband's brother, Peregrine Marsh, and his wife, the former Lady Henrietta Pringle, were both killed, she and William raised their two small daughters, Penelope and Daphne, as their own. Lady Elizabeth gazed fondly across the room at her husband.

Lord William Marsh, the 8th Duke of Hunsford, was a kind, portly, blustering man. He puffed on his

pipe while reading his newspaper. His trusty compan-
ion, Cuddles, a Cavalier King Charles spaniel, slept by
his feet. Lord William not only looked the part of the
lord of the manor, but he was also the quintessential
old country squire.

The door to the drawing room opened, and
Thompkins, the Marsh family's prim and proper butler, entered. He stood erect, gave a discreet cough,
and announced, "Reverend Baker and Lady Amelia
Dallyripple."

"Time I made my escape," Lord William whispered, and rose.

Lady Elizabeth barely had time to frown her disapproval at her husband before Thompkins returned
with the unlikely pair in tow.

Thwarted, Lord William huffed and returned to
his seat.

Lady Elizabeth frowned. She'd expected a visit
from Lady Amelia sooner or later. Still, she had hoped
it would be later. Much later. Lady Amelia was a determined woman accustomed to getting her way. She
hadn't been pleased when the Marshes declined her
request to host the annual village fete. However,
Lady Elizabeth hadn't expected that she would seek
the aid of the vicar in getting her way.

Lady Amelia Dallyripple was a large horsey-faced
woman. She usually had a swarm of corgis circling
her legs and nipping at the heels of her guests.

Reverend Baker was a small, studious man with
kind eyes. As he was normally not one to take sides in
village politics, Lady Elizabeth was stunned to see
that Lady Dallyripple had enlisted his help in further-
ing her agenda. Perhaps more stunning, or disappointing, was the fact that the vicar had come.

The visitors settled in, and the group exchanged pleasantries. The unseasonably warm weather for late autumn was a safe topic. They had just about exhausted the subject when Thompkins entered with a heavily laden tea tray. He placed the tray onto a cart and wheeled it beside Lady Elizabeth. After helping to serve the sandwiches, tarts, and fine pastries, he distributed the tea and then quietly made his exit.

After a brief moment of silence, Lady Amelia leaned forward. "I'm sure you know why I'm here. It's time we get this business settled once and for all."

Lady Elizabeth sipped her tea. "Honestly, Amelia, I thought it was settled. Given the state of the nation, we just don't feel it would be right to host a fete on the very brink of war."

"That's just why we need to have the fete, and the vicar agrees with me." Lady Amelia turned to face the vicar. "Don't you?"

The vicar tugged at his collar and took a deep breath. "As you know, I normally try to stay out of village disputes. Wickfield Lodge is your estate and your home, and I wouldn't dream of trying to influence you."

Lady Amelia huffed.

"However, I feel that I would be remiss in my role as spiritual advisor to the village if I didn't share my humble opinion."

"Certainly, Vicar," Lady Elizabeth said. "We are always open to other views, and we greatly value your opinion."

Reverend Baker smiled. "First, I want to be completely honest and share my personal, perhaps selfish reason for wanting to have the fete." He took a deep breath. "As you know, the funds raised from the fete go toward the church building fund, and we are sorely in need of a new roof. The carpenters assure me that we will not survive another year without a new roof."

The state of the church's roof was an established fact. The Ladies Aid Society had been canvassing the parish to collect money to replace the roof, but their efforts had fallen far short. Lady Elizabeth planned to talk to her husband about making a large donation to ensure the roof was repaired, but with all of the excitement about the baby, she hadn't gotten around to it yet. She listened to the vicar's argument.

"My second and perhaps more important reason for asking you to reconsider is that I feel you're right. It won't be long before our nation will once again be at war with Germany." He paused and shook his head. "Who knows the devastation that will have. Our brave men will answer the call of their country. Many of our local lads will go and perhaps not return. Our women will also do their duty as they did in the last war and throughout our nation's history. This fete may seem insignificant when compared to war, but as one who's served my country, I can assure you that it isn't. When our men find themselves in trenches miles from English soil in enemy territory, it is those memories that keep them sane. Memories of family and friends. Of times spent sharing laughter, food and drink, games, and, yes, I think time spent at a village fete during peaceful times. That's what you remember. It's those memories that remind you just what you're fighting for . . . why you're there. This may be the last time that we can all come together to create those memories for our young people. Our last chance before—" The vicar's voice caught from emotion.

Even Lord William coughed and blustered more than usual as he puffed on his pipe.

Lady Elizabeth pulled a handkerchief from her sleeve and dabbed at her eyes. She glanced at her husband, who gave a brief nod.

"We hadn't thought of it from that side before," Lady Elizabeth said, "but you're right."

"If hosting a village fete will boost morale for our young men, then by God we'll do it," Lord William said and then quickly blew his nose.

The vicar bowed his head in appreciation.

Lady Amelia sat up in her seat and smiled. "Good. I'm glad that's settled."

If Lady Elizabeth wondered what Amelia Dallyripple's goal in pushing for the fete was, she didn't have long to wait.

"I knew you'd come to your senses sooner or later. That's why *I* haven't been stagnant, watching the grass grow under my feet. I've managed to secure Colonel Basil Livingston as our guest of honor to open the fete." She gazed at the others expectantly. When she received nothing but blank stares in response, she said, "Don't tell me you haven't heard of Colonel Livingston?"

"Dr. Livingston, I presume?" Lord William laughed. "Only Livingston I've heard about."

Reverend Baker grinned at the joke.

Lady Amelia was not amused. She mumbled something that sounded like "uncultured Neanderthals." "Basil, I mean Colonel Livingston, distinguished himself in the Great War. He's won a ton of medals and commendations. Later, when he returned home, he wrote a book about his time in the military. Colonel Livingston has rented a cottage in the village to work on his latest book, which he claims will be an eye-opening look inside the military."

"Bosh!" Lord William slammed his fist on the arm of his chair, scattering tobacco from his pipe onto the rug and startling Cuddles awake.

"William!" Lady Elizabeth said.

"Sorry, dear, but that just gets my back up. Our country is about to go to war. The last thing we need is some old duffer trying to make himself important by sharing our military secrets with the world. Why, the Nazis won't need to send spies to infiltrate our military. They just need to swing down to their local newsstand and drop a crown or two."

Reverend Baker looked as though he had sucked a lemon.

Lady Amelia sat straighter and taller. "Well, I don't know about that, but I think the publicity will bring people to our fete in droves." She turned to the vicar. "Don't you agree, Vicar?"

Caught in the middle of yet another political debate, Reverend Baker took off his spectacles and shined them. "People do seem to like books about scandal. However, I would hope that no Englishman, especially a military man, would print anything that would betray our nation."

Lord William seethed in silence.

Lady Amelia refused to be daunted by the poor reception for her guest of honor. Instead, she smiled the look of a woman with a secret. "Well, I think it'll be a huge success. And I have one other piece of news." She grinned. "I've finally had enough of Charlotte Granger's moods, always raving on about one grievance after another. The other servants and I were always walking on eggshells, trying to not upset her and ignoring her threats to leave every few days if she didn't get her way about something. Well, I had enough. This time when she had hysterics and threatened to quit, I accepted." Lady Amelia took a bite of the orange marmalade cake and frowned.

Lady Elizabeth knew that the frown was not because of a flaw in the cake. The Marshes' cook, Mrs. Anderson, was a brilliant baker. Her cake was moist and delicate with just the right balance of orange and spice. It was everything a cake should be. No, Lady Amelia's frown was rooted in the fact that try as she might, she could find nothing wrong with the cake. It was delicious.

"You can't mean to say you've sacked the poor woman?" Lady Elizabeth asked.

"I do mean it. I tell you, I've had enough."

"But Charlotte Granger is a wonderful cook. Sure, she's temperamental, but most good cooks are. She's been with you for years. Plus, she's local." Lady Elizabeth prided herself on keeping an open mind, but when it came to the village and its inhabitants, her alliances were clear.

"Humph. I'm sure she won't have a problem finding another situation. I've given her a month's severance and a glowing letter of reference." Lady Amelia's smile indicated there was more that she wasn't sharing.

"Servants . . . good help is hard to find," Lady Elizabeth said. "It's not like in years past when families stayed in domestic service for generations. Now, young people have opportunities. Plus, with the war looming, many women will want to do their bit to help. They'll join the Women's Army Auxiliary Corps, the Women's Royal Naval Service, Auxiliary Territorial Service, and the Red Cross. You'll never be able to find anyone half as good to replace her."

"Good help isn't as hard to find as you'd think. *If* you know where to look."

"Where?"

"France. Paris to be specific. I've already engaged Monsieur Jean Luc Baill. He graduated at the top of his class from Paris's famous Le Cordon Bleu. Your Mrs. Anderson won't have such an easy time winning the baking trophy at the fete this year. This time, she'll have some real competition."

Chapter 4

My cell phone chimed, bringing me back from the English countryside to the here and now. One glance at my phone showed the message was from Frank. He was running a little late but would be there within thirty minutes.

I rushed to take a quick shower and hurried to get dressed. I thought more than once about changing my mind and skipping the dinner, but the phrase *imposter syndrome* floated through my head. Nana Jo would never let me live it down if I didn't go. Besides, I'd spent a small fortune on the black-beaded, sequined dress, and opportunities to wear anything quite that fancy were limited in North Harbor, Michigan. I even went all out and put on a pair of pantyhose.

Frank arrived in less than his thirty-minute estimate. His face told me that he appreciated the extra effort I'd put into my appearance. He whistled. "Are you sure you want to go out tonight? We could just stay home."

"Don't tempt me. I'd like nothing better than to put on a comfy pair of yoga pants and a sweatshirt and cuddle up with you and a bowl of popcorn, but I gave my word."

"You really don't want to go?"

"No."

"Then don't." He loosened his tie. "You're an adult. You don't have to go if you don't want to."

"Don't go filling her head with that tomfoolery," Nana Jo said, stomping upstairs. "You're just enabling her insecurities and feeding into her imposter syndrome."

"Imposter syndrome?" Frank glanced from me to Nana Jo.

"Never mind," I said. "I'll explain it on the way to the banquet." I straightened Frank's tie, grabbed my purse, and let him help me on with my jacket.

Frank always parked his car next to the bookstore's side door. The driveway led beside the bookstore and between the bookstore and the parking lot that I shared with the church next door. He drove a black Porsche Cayenne with soft Italian leather seats.

The drive to MISU's campus was short, and I took the time to fill Frank in on the events from earlier today, including Nana Jo's diagnosis of my condition.

When we got to the campus, Frank turned to me. "You don't have to go if you don't want to. Say the word and we can be in front of a nice fire sipping wine and eating the most delicious coquilles St.-Jacques you've ever eaten."

"It would have to be." I grinned. "I'm pretty sure I've never had it before. What is it?"

"Scallops."

"Thank you, but I need to do this—I want to do it. I've dreamed about being a published author for years, and now, here it is. I'm published. I've got to take the good with the bad. It's not just the thrill of seeing my book in print on bookshelves or hearing from readers who enjoyed the book. It's the bad reviews from people who hated my book and tag me on social media to tell me how much they hated it. The one-star reviews from people who were upset because they ordered the book and it arrived late or damaged by the postal service.

It's all of that together." I took a deep breath. "It's even being at a book festival with people who think cozies are 'cute' and lightweight. It's all part of the package, right?"

Frank reached over and squeezed my hand. "Whatever happens, I'm here with you."

He dropped me as close to the door as possible and then parked the car while I waited for him inside the building. He was back quickly. He gave my hand another squeeze and escorted me into the main banquet room.

One of the conference rooms had been converted into a banquet room by the addition of round tables facing an elevated stage. Just inside the doors was a table where several students that I'd noticed earlier sat checking names off a list and handing out name tags.

Inside, dozens of round tables with numbers were set with china place settings, shiny silverware, and sparkling crystal glasses. The left front corner of the room had been cordoned off and set up as a bar.

Frank stopped a waiter carrying a tray with two glasses. He handed one to me and took one for himself. We meandered around the outskirts of the room, looking for a familiar face.

"Oh no," I mumbled to Frank. "Scarlet MacDunkin at three o'clock."

Frank casually sipped his champagne and stole a glance in the direction I mentioned.

"Hi there," Scarlet said. "Came back for more torment?" She cackled. "I'm glad to see you weren't scared away by the infighting earlier. I was half afraid that our lone cozy writer wouldn't come back."

"Scared?" I said. "Why would I be scared?"

"Sam's pretty tough," Frank said. "It'll take a lot more than a few badly behaved authors to scare her away."

If I wasn't already madly in love with him, those comments would have won me over.

"Scarlet, this is my fiancé, Frank Patterson. Frank, this is Scarlet MacDunkin."

Scarlet extended a hand, and the two shook. She flashed a bright smile and gazed adoringly at Frank. "Aren't you handsome. It's a pleasure to meet you. Are you an author too?"

"No. I'm just a cook and a mystery reader." Frank extracted his hand and put a possessive arm around my waist.

"Actually, Frank's being modest," I said. "He owns an extremely popular restaurant in downtown North Harbor."

"What types of mysteries do you like to read? Wait, let me guess." Scarlet ogled Frank as though she were evaluating a prize heifer at the county fair. "A big, strong man like you, you look like you'd like a good thriller or a police procedural."

"I do enjoy thrillers. I recently read *They Come at Knight* by Yasmin Angoe. But now my interests have shifted, and I have to say that I'm in love with cozy mysteries." Frank gazed at me.

Scarlet got the hint. She took a step back, stopped batting her eyelashes, and took a sip of her champagne. "Yes. Well, then you two are certainly well suited."

We were just about to walk away when Scarlet gasped and grabbed my arm. "You can't leave now. Things are about to get really interesting."

I followed her gaze to a couple that had just entered the room. The man was tall, dark, slender, and handsome. Too handsome. Not a hair out of place, with teeth that were blindingly white. Even from a distance, I could tell they were perfectly straight. The woman hanging on his arm was a contradiction in terms. In some ways, she was small. She had a slim figure, a small waistline, and a small heart-shaped face. She was small in stature, but she made up for it with superhigh heels, which Nana Jo referred to as "hooker heels." They were at least six inches, but she marched in them like a boss.

In other ways, she was over the top. Her blond hair was teased like cotton candy piled atop her head. It was an ode to the 1980s and added six more inches to her height. But the biggest things were by far her bust and lips. Neither of which were natural.

Scarlet grabbed another glass of champagne from a passing waiter and stood with a gleeful gleam in her eyes. "Good Lord, her lips look like Mick Jagger's, and get a look at those watermelons."

"Who are they?" I asked.

"The hunk is bestselling author Paul West. The life-sized Barbie doll draped across his arm is his wife, Olivia Townsend."

"Paul West? He writes spy novels. I have some of his books in my store. I seem to remember reading something about him and Judith Hunter, but if he's married, I must have him confused with someone else."

"Oh no. You're not confused." Scarlet smiled. "Judith and Paul had a wild fling. Rumor has it he was all set to leave his wife and start over with Judith. That is until Judith dumped him and he came scurrying back to his wife like a lost puppy with his tail tucked between his legs. Judith found someone who could do more for her career than Paul."

Something about Scarlet's voice sounded uncharacteristically sad. I stole a glance at her, and for a brief moment, her hard shell cracked, and I glimpsed her soft interior. But it didn't last long.

Scarlet tossed back her champagne and grabbed another glass. "Out with the old and in with the new. Olivia's an author too. She writes charming middle-grade mysteries. Word on the street is that the breakup sent her over the edge. She had a nervous breakdown. This is the first time she's been seen out in public in months." She sipped her champagne.

"That's horrible. I hope she's better, but . . ." I looked around the room.

"But won't seeing Judith be upsetting for the poor dear? Gawd, I hope so." Scarlet cackled and drank her champagne.

I scanned the room for a familiar face that I could latch onto and get away from Scarlet MacDunkin. Anyone would be better than standing here. That's when I spotted Nora Cooper.

I gasped.

Scarlet must have seen her too because her face lit up like a Christmas tree. "Oh, this is going to be fantastic." She lifted her arm and waved. "Nora, over here."

Nora Cooper sauntered over. Apart from being a bit flushed, she seemed practically giddy.

"Scarlet." Nora turned to face me, and I could tell she didn't remember my name. "You're that cozy mystery writer."

"Samantha Washington, and this is my fiancé, Frank Patterson."

"I didn't expect to see you here tonight," Scarlet said. "I thought Judith had you thrown out."

I had to give Scarlet credit for saying what I was thinking but lacked both the courage and venom to say.

"Ha! I'd like to see her try," Nora said a tad bit too loudly. "I paid for my registration, and I'm entitled to stay." Her face was flushed, and it was obvious that she was more than a little tipsy.

Paul West and his wife passed by.

"Oh, this is going to be fun." Scarlet leaned close. "That's Paul West and his life-sized Barbie doll, Olivia."

The couple nodded and kept walking, intent on continuing on, but Scarlet wasn't going to let that happen.

"Paul, do you know Samantha Washington? She's a local

author and newest cozy mystery sensation." Scarlet grinned. "And her handsome fiancé."

Paul and Frank shook hands.

"And, this is Olivia Townsend. Olivia writes middle-grade mysteries featuring a middle-school magician. You used to be one of those magician assistants that got sawed in half. Didn't you?" Scarlet asked.

"Magician assistant, voice actor, author, you name it, I did it." Olivia blushed.

The tension was intense, but good manners merited at least a pretense of civility.

I turned to Paul West. "I also own a mystery bookshop, and your spy novels are always popular with my local readers. If you find yourself in downtown North Harbor, I'd love it if you came by and signed stock copies." One thing I'd learned since having my book published was that authors loved signing stock. Readers liked buying signed copies of books and authors loved that once the books were signed, bookstores rarely returned unsold copies.

Paul West flashed his perfect smile. "I can see you have a discerning readership in this town."

I gave him a business card with the store's address. I turned to the other authors. "I'm pretty sure I have at least one of all of your books. Or I did before the book festival started. I can't make any guarantees now. They've been flying off the shelves like hotcakes. But you're all welcome to sign stock as well."

Scarlet waylaid a waiter with a full tray of champagne and handed glasses all around. "Let's all drink to Sam's bookstore and signing stock."

I'd barely touched my champagne, so I declined. However, when everyone had a full glass, Scarlet lifted hers in a toast. "To Sam."

"To Sam," everyone repeated and sipped their champagne.

I could feel the heat rising up my neck as I tried to re-member my Emily Post. *If you're the honoree of a toast, are you sup-posed to drink?* I didn't think so, which was fine with me, since I am not a big alcohol drinker, and the last time I had champagne, I may have made an utter and complete fool of myself.

However, what I didn't drink, Nora Cooper and Paul West made up for. Both tossed back their drinks and quickly grabbed another before the waiter could get too far away.

It was clear from Paul West's slurred speech that he was well on his way to total inebriation. With each drink, his safe-guards went down. He grew louder and more uninhibited. And if I didn't know better, I'd say Scarlet MacDunkin was deliberately making sure that neither Paul's nor Nora's glass was empty for long.

Up close and personal, Olivia Townsend appeared strained. When I indicated that it was time Frank and I made our way around the room, Olivia latched onto my arm and held on for dear life.

"Oh, please stay. I really want to hear more about your bookstore, but first, tell me about *Murder at Wickfield Lodge*. I loved your book. I loved Lady Elizabeth, and I think Thomp-kins is lovely. In particular, I loved the quaint English village. Is it based on a real location?"

Oh my God! Olivia Townsend had actually read my book. She knew character names and hadn't just skimmed the back cover. We chatted, and I learned that she was a huge fan of British historical mysteries. Olivia drew Frank into the con-versation too, which further endeared her to me.

The group split into two subgroups of three. The group of Olivia, Frank, and me discussed books, England, and the nu-ances leading up to World War II in Great Britain.

The other group of Scarlet, Nora, and Paul West drank quite a few more glasses of champagne. As they drank, their volume increased. Inevitably, Judith Hunter's name came up.

Even without being an active participant in the group, I knew that Scarlet MacDunkin steered the conversation. She was what Nana Jo called "a pot stirrer." She had stirred up Paul and Nora to the point where they were ready to boil over.

"Judith Hunter couldn't plot her way out of a brown paper bag," Paul West said. He knocked back his champagne as if he were taking shots of tequila and accepted the replacement that Scarlet handed him.

Nora Cooper held up her newly filled glass in salute. "Hear, hear."

Paul and Nora clinked glasses and drank.

"She got lucky with *The Corpse Danced at Midnight*," Paul West said. He waved his arm and sloshed his drink, spilling most of it on Nora, but she didn't mind.

"Lucky? She stole it. That's my book. I wrote every word of it. And Little Miss Bestseller Judith Hunter is going to get the rug pulled out from under her feet. Then she won't be the darling of the crime fiction circuit." Nora laughed hysterically.

"The only reason she's so popular is because she's got everyone fooled," Paul West said too loudly. "She flashes that big, fake smile and turns on the sex appeal. I would love to wipe that smile off her face."

Frank leaned close and whispered, "Isn't that Judith Hunter?" He inclined his head slightly.

Sure enough, Judith Hunter and Clark Cunningham were standing less than three feet from us. There was no way they hadn't heard those comments.

The red rash rising up Judith's neck proved her hearing was sound.

Clark Cunningham approached the group. "Hello, Paul. I think you've had more than enough to drink tonight. Why don't you go and sleep it off before you say something you'll regret."

"Regret? The only thing I regret is that I was fooled by that little . . . tramp." Paul pointed toward Judith.

Clark Cunningham made eye contact with one of the students standing by the door and beckoned him over.

"Clark, you can't do that," Olivia pleaded.

"What's the matter?" Nora said. "Afraid of a little straight talk?"

"Paul is one of the presenters, and he's nominated for the Best Spy Thriller," Olivia said. "You can't remove him. Not now." She glanced from Clark to Judith. "You're doing this for her. She's determined to destroy Paul."

The student arrived, and Clark Cunningham whispered something to him. The student hurried away, returning within moments with two security guards.

The noise level in the banquet room had gone down, and all eyes were directed toward our group.

The security guards moved on either side of Paul West, but he had no intention of going quietly. As one of the guards grabbed him by the arm, West hauled back and took a swing at him.

Perhaps in his younger days and when he wasn't drunk, he might have connected. Instead, the security guard merely leaned back, and the punch missed. Momentum mixed with nearly a bottle of champagne caused West to lose his balance. He stumbled to the ground.

The security guards helped him to his feet and propelled him out the nearest door.

Olivia fumed. "You didn't need to do that. You didn't need to humiliate him like that." She tossed her drink in Clark Cunningham's face. She lunged at Judith Hunter, but even with a face dripping with champagne, Clark Cunningham was able to tackle her before she got to Judith Hunter.

Judith spilled a bit of champagne and dropped her purse, but was otherwise unscathed.

Olivia's parting shot included a few words that would never be allowed in a middle-grade mystery and marched out the door after her husband.

Scarlet burst out laughing.

Nora Cooper pointed at Judith. "You think you're the queen of the ball, well, I have a surprise plot twist for your Cinderella story. Your Prince Charming can't save you this time. In fact, Prince Charming may just be the one who puts that final nail in your coffin."

"Nora, that's enough," Clark Cunningham said.

"Enough? Oh no, I've only begun to fight." Nora shoved her drink at Judith.

Judith Hunter had been holding both her drink and Cunningham's while he braced himself for battle with Paul West. She placed one drink on a nearby table and offered Cunningham a handkerchief.

Clark wiped his face and then glanced around the room.

The crowd sensed that the excitement was over, and everyone returned to their conversations.

"You look like you could use a drink," Judith said, glancing at the various glasses of champagne on the table. "I don't know which glass belongs to whom anymore. Here, take mine." She handed Cunningham her glass and turned to a waiter and got another glass of champagne for herself. She held up the glass. "Cheers."

"Cheers," everyone repeated and took a sip.

Clark Cunningham made a loud gurgling sound. He clutched at his throat.

"Clark, what's wrong?" Nora asked.

His eyes bulged, and he clawed at his throat. Eventually, he collapsed.

Frank knelt next to him and loosened Cunningham's tie and collar. "Call nine-one-one."

I fumbled to get my cell out of my purse and push the numbers on my phone.

A stylish Black woman with a red pillbox hat who was standing nearby rushed over and knelt down. "I'm Dr. Gordon." She checked his pulse and examined his pupils. "Do you have any medical conditions? Allergies?"

Clark Cunningham glanced at her, but then his entire body began to shake. It wasn't clear if his shakes were in response to her questions or a reaction to whatever had happened to him.

The shakes became more intense until he was convulsing violently.

"Should we hold him down?" Frank asked.

"This is real life, not fiction," Dr. Gordon said. "You shouldn't bother someone having a seizure."

"Put something in his mouth so he doesn't swallow his tongue," Nora said. "That's what they do in books."

Dr. Gordon scowled. "He won't swallow his tongue, and biting it is the least of his worries right now. Did he take any medications? Eat or drink anything?"

We turned to look at Judith.

"No . . . at least, I don't think so. He used to have a problem with drugs, but he's been clean for months. The only thing he had was some champagne . . . my champagne."

After a few seconds, the convulsions stopped.

"Nine-one-one. What's your emergency?"

Chapter 5

"Someone should go and direct the EMTs here," Dr. Gordon said, focusing on me.

Going to meet the ambulance was the best suggestion anyone could have given me. In that moment, there was nothing that I wanted more than to get out of that room, and I fled as quickly as I could.

I hurried out the door and down the hall to the main entrance while answering as many questions as I could from the 9-1-1 dispatcher, which wasn't much.

The sound of sirens grew louder, and I eventually saw the flashing lights as the ambulance sped to a stop.

I hung up with the 9-1-1 dispatcher and led the EMTs to the banquet hall.

The hallway, which was relatively clear earlier, was now crammed. Someone had cleared everyone out of the banquet room, and they were all crowded into the hallway.

The EMTs flung open the door and hurried to the area where Clark Cunningham lay on the floor.

Dr. Gordon, her hat slightly askew, stood and talked to the EMTs, who quickly got busy working on Cunningham.

Standing near the back wall, Scarlet MacDunkin held Nora Cooper, who was trembling and sobbing. She was on the verge of hysterics.

Within minutes, the EMTs had Cunningham on a gurney with oxygen and were rushing him out of the room and down the hall.

Not being family, Judith Hunter wasn't allowed in the ambulance, but she said she would follow in her car, and rushed after them.

"Sam."

I scanned the room until I saw Frank standing near a tray of discarded champagne glasses. One glass lay on the floor.

One look into his eyes told me something wasn't right.

"What's wrong?" *Other than the fact that we just watched a man have a seizure and nearly die? Geez!* That would be enough to rattle anyone. In fact, I couldn't wait until we were alone, and I could have a complete breakdown in the comfort and privacy of my own home. But that was me, former high school English teacher turned bookstore owner and author. Frank was different. He was former military and didn't rattle easily. He'd seen *and done* things that he said he kept buried deep down inside and locked behind a mental door that he never dared open, because if he ever did, it would take him out. I gazed at the man I loved and tried to read what was going on behind the invisible wall he created around his emotions, but he was good. Barely a crack showed, but still there was something.

He said, "I think you should call Stinky Pitt."

Chapter 6

Stinky Pitt was the unfortunate nickname that Detective Bradley Pitt had been saddled with in elementary school. Nana Jo had been his second grade math teacher and remembered the nickname whenever she wanted to torment the detective. We rarely used the name in public, so Frank's choice to use it now meant he didn't want anyone else to know I was calling the police.

Detective Pitt was a detective in the Special Crimes Unit of the North Harbor Police. Our paths had crossed many times. He wasn't what I would call a friend, but thankfully I wouldn't classify him as an enemy . . . well, not anymore. To say that Detective Pitt viewed me as little more than a nuisance was an understatement. However, I did help save him from going to jail for a murder he didn't commit. And now that he was officially back to work, he'd practically forgiven me for being the cause of his getting shot.

Frank knew all of this, so if he was suggesting that I call Detective Pitt, something was *definitely* not right.

I nodded and swiped my phone until I found the number

I wanted. Then, I stepped away to a quiet corner where my conversation wouldn't be overheard.

"Mrs. Washington, to what do I owe this pleasure?" Sarcasm dripped from Detective Pitt's every word.

I pulled the phone away from my ear and childishly stuck my tongue out at him. "I'm at MISU for the book festival awards banquet, and something bad happened. You need to get here."

"What happened? Please don't tell me someone was murdered."

"I don't know if he's dead . . . yet. The EMTs took him off to the hospital, but he didn't look good. I was—"

"Who?"

"His name's Clark Cunningham. He's a publicist, but I don't—"

"Are you telling me someone tried to kill this man in the middle of some kind of banquet?"

"Look. If you'd stop interrupting me, I could tell you what I know, which isn't much."

The line went quiet, so I quickly filled Detective Pitt in. When I finished, the line was still silent.

"Are you still there?" I asked.

"Just waiting for you to finish."

"I'm done."

"Good. Now, I know I'm going to regret asking this, but what makes you think a crime has been committed? Based on what little information you've told me, it doesn't sound like it to me. How do you know that he didn't have an allergic reaction to something, maybe peanuts or shellfish? You and that crazy grandmother of yours have murder on the brain. You're like murder magnets. Someone has appendicitis and immediately you're claiming they've been poisoned."

I glanced at Frank.

His eyes asked, *What's taking so long?*

I rolled my eyes and held up my phone.

Frank beckoned for me. When I got there, he took the phone and listened for a few seconds before interrupting. "Detective Pitt, Frank Patterson. Cunningham'll never make it to the hospital alive. I told Sam to call because when I knelt beside him, I smelled bitter almonds on his breath. In less than ten minutes, someone's going to send us all home. Now, I'm standing here protecting the evidence—the champagne glass he drank from before he convulsed and dropped to the ground. If you don't want your crime scene destroyed by two hundred people and a host of college students pretending to be waiters, then stop arguing and get over here, now."

Chapter 7

At the front of the room, Mrs. Graves and Dr. Peters had been having an intense conversation that would have made the Camp David peace talks look like a comedy. When they finished, they moved on stage, and Dr. Peters took the microphone and requested everyone return to the ballroom.

Slowly, the crowds in the hallway made their way back into the banquet room.

"We have all just witnessed a terrible tragedy," Dr. Peters said. "Our hearts and prayers go out to Clark Cunningham and his family. We are praying that he will recover from this unfortunate event quickly and will once again be able to join us to celebrate books and the authors that he loved."

There was tepid applause from the audience.

"In the meantime, I'm sure you would all agree that it would be . . . disrespectful to continue the banquet tonight. So, with the gracious help of the university, we're going to postpone our banquet. We will post—"

"Hold it right there." Detective Bradley Pitt and a small army burst through the doors and rushed into the banquet room. With one arm in the air holding his shield up for all the world to see, Detective Pitt scurried to the front of the room.

Clad in polyester pants that were too short and too tight, a polyester shirt that was too snug, and a balding dome with a bad comb-over, Detective Bradley Pitt climbed the two steps to the stage and took the microphone from Dr. Peters.

"Detective Bradley Pitt. North Harbor Police."

"Police?" Mrs. Graves said. "Are you saying that Clark Cunningham . . . that he—"

"Clark Cunningham died en route to the hospital."

There was a murmur from the crowd.

"That's tragic. Truly tragic, but why are you here? Are you implying that his death wasn't an accident?"

Mrs. Graves was a smart cookie. She had pieced together the facts in record time and come up with the right conclusion.

"That's exactly what I'm saying."

A louder murmur rose from the crowd.

"That's impossible," Mrs. Graves said. "This was a tragic and unfortunate accident. You're—"

"I'm saying this is an official police investigation. No one is to leave until you have given your name, address, and contact information to Officer Martinez." He looked up. "Officer Martinez, wave your hand."

An officer at the back of the room waved his hand.

"Anyone with direct knowledge of the incident should see Officer Hopewell. Officer Hopewell?"

A young, uniformed woman waved her hand.

"It's going to be a long night, but we appreciate your cooperation." Detective Pitt turned and left the stage amid a murmur that sounded like a mob prepared to revolt.

He made a beeline for Frank and me. When he arrived, he scowled at me. "You. I should have known you can't even go

to a fancy banquet without getting involved in a murder investigation." He looked around. "At least you don't have the
rest of the nosy old biddies with you."

He'd better be grateful that Nana Jo wasn't here for
that one.

"Wait," Frank said. "This isn't Sam's fault. She barely knew
Cunningham."

Detective Pitt snorted.

"Is he really dead?" I asked.

Pitt nodded. "Now, what can you tell me?"

Frank and I filled him in on what we'd seen. When we
finished, the scowl from the start of our conversation was full
and intense. "You mean he didn't drink out of his own glass?"

We shook our heads.

"The poison had—"

"So it was poison?" I asked. "Cyanide?"

"That's what we're thinking. Won't know for sure until
the toxicology tests come back." He frowned and said grudg-
ingly, "Thanks to your fiancé here, we have a lead. Might not
have been able to get a handle on this without the heads-up.
But, keep it under your hat. We won't be releasing that to the
public."

A photographer snapped pictures, placing numbered mark-
ers around everything that could possibly be related to the
crime scene. A forensic investigator dusted and bagged the
glass.

The officer who waved her hand and identified herself as
Officer Hopewell whispered in Detective Pitt's ear. When she
finished, Detective Pitt glanced around the banquet room.

The crowd stood around watching the police. Most had
their cell phones out taking pictures or videotaping.

"What're they doing?" Detective Pitt said. "Usually, when
I tell a room full of potential suspects they can't leave, there's a

huge uproar. We get called every name you can imagine. *You can't do this. Violating my civil rights.* Yadda. Yadda. You would think I'd asked them to sacrifice their firstborn or something. Not this group. Only about twenty people have tried to leave. The rest are all standing around taking pictures like tourists. What's with these weirdos?"

I smiled. "I'll bet this is the first time you've had a murder in a room full of authors. A few even write crime fiction."

"You mean they're taking pictures so they can write a book about it?" Detective Pitt glared at me.

"Opportunities like this don't come around every day," I said, immediately regretting it. "Thank goodness."

Detective Pitt frowned and mumbled something that sounded like *nut jobs.*

On a good day, Detective Pitt was cocky, arrogant, and resistant to my help. Getting called out to a potential murder meant today was *not* a good day. His face was red as he choked, "So, what can you tell me?"

Asking for help, especially from me, had to hurt. I hesitated. I felt sympathetic for a few moments.

"Come on, Nancy Drew. You and your grandmother are too nosy not to have picked up some dirt on this lot."

All of the sympathy I felt moments earlier seeped out of my body.

"Tell him about what you heard," Frank said.

"I knew it. I knew you would have gotten some dirt. Spill it."

I took a deep breath and shared the conversation I'd overheard earlier. When I finished, I shared the comments from Paul West.

Detective Pitt scowled. "I don't get it. So, Nora Cooper and Scarlet MacDunkin were both angry with Judith Hunter. What's that got to do with Clark Cunningham?"

"Don't you see?" I asked.

Detective Pitt shook his head.

"It wasn't his drink," Frank said. "Clark Cunningham spilled his drink. Judith Hunter gave Cunningham her glass."

"So, if the poison was in the glass of champagne that Clark Cunningham drank," I said, "then he wasn't the intended victim."

Detective Pitt whipped out his cell phone and took a few steps away to a corner.

I looked over at the table where Nora Cooper and Scarlet MacDunkin were seated. Both women were staring at me. I turned so my back was to the women and I was facing Frank. "Have they been watching us the entire time?"

"Yup."

I glanced in their direction and then quickly averted my eyes when I spotted a gleeful look in Scarlet's. *Holy cow. She wants to talk.* Head high. Keep my gaze moving. Sadly, nothing will make you do something more than deliberately trying not to do it. The more I dodged eye contact, the more I felt my eyes drawn to the two women. Eventually, I lost the battle. I locked eyes with Scarlet MacDunkin and had no choice but to acknowledge her wave to join them.

"Crap," I whispered.

Frank smiled. "Do you need me to run interference?"

"No," I huffed.

"Just remember the three keys to tactical conversation survival."

I plastered on a smile and walked over to the table. I opened my mouth to speak but didn't get a chance.

"You have an inside track with that cop," Scarlet said. "Spill it. What's going on?"

"Actually, I'm not that friendly with Detective Pitt. In fact, he dislikes me . . . a *lot*." *Tactical conversation survival point number one—avoidance.* I latched onto one thing and hoped neither of the women would notice that I avoided the conversation. I should have known it wouldn't work.

"Was Clark Cunningham really murdered?" Nora whispered.

"I don't know. There must have been something suspicious, or he wouldn't be here, right?" *Tactical conversation survival point number two—answer a question with a question.* That didn't work either.

"Who would want to kill Clark Cunningham?" Nora asked.

Tactical conversation survival point number three—diversion. "Squirrel."

"Excuse me?" Nora said.

"Girl—that *girl* . . . I mean, *woman* over there." I pointed to the door. "Isn't that Judith?"

Their gazes followed the direction of my finger to a crowd that was gathered near the door. In the center of the gathering, the crown of a blond head was visible.

"Oh, goody," Scarlet said. Her eyes held a mischievous glint. "Things are about to get really interesting now."

"What do you mean?" Nora asked.

"With any luck, maybe the murderer will make another attempt now that the real target is back."

Chapter 8

"You can't be serious," Nora said.

Scarlet rolled her eyes. "Don't be a fool. Anyone with half of a brain cell can see that Judith was the intended victim, not Clark Cunningham. Who would want to kill a wimp like that with the queen of the shrews standing right there?"

Detective Pitt finished his telephone conversation and came up to our group.

He looked at Scarlet and Nora. "Names."

I frowned and concentrated all of my mental energy on sending a telepathic message to Detective Pitt, but either my telepathy wasn't working or the detective didn't have the intuitive powers that God gave to a fruit fly.

The ladies complied, and Detective Pitt wrote their names in his notebook, barely taking a minute to glance up at them.

"Were you present when Mr. Cunningham drank the champagne and had a fit? Did you see anyone lingering nearby who shouldn't have been there?"

Both women relayed much of the same story that I had, but being fiction writers, they elaborated on the tale, making it far more sinister than had been the case. Scarlet was sure that the waiter she'd gotten the drinks from was someone she'd seen earlier in the day skulking around the auditorium and casting suspicious glances at Judith Hunter.

Nora didn't recognize the waiter, but then she hadn't been trying. One college student in black pants and a white shirt carrying a tray of champagne looked just like another one. However, she did feel an eerie presence right before Clark Cunningham drank the champagne. She was especially sensitive to auras, and she had seen a dark cloud hovering over him.

Detective Pitt looked up from his notebook.

I gave up on mental telepathy. "Detective, these are the two women I was telling you about earlier. You were going to interview them about Judith Hunter."

He tore his glance away from Nora and frowned. "What are you babbling about? You're almost as bad as that crazy grandmother of yours."

I sighed.

Dr. Leonard Peters, microphone in hand, hurried over to our small group, with a student hoisting a heavy camera on his shoulder following close behind. The student turned on a light that nearly blinded me while Dr. Peters thrust the microphone in front of Detective Pitt's face. "Detective Pitt, is it true that Clark Cunningham was not the intended victim here tonight?"

I wasn't sure, but it sounded as though Dr. Peters's voice had dropped an octave or two since the panel discussion he'd facilitated earlier.

Detective Pitt froze and stared into the camera's light as though hypnotized. "Huh?"

"There's a rumor going around that Clark Cunningham may not have been the killer's intended victim. Can you corroborate that?"

"What?"

"What are the North Harbor Police doing to protect Judith Hunter?" Dr. Peters asked.

One well-placed elbow and Scarlet MacDunkin shoved her way in front of the camera. She flashed a big smile. "Oh, Leonard. I thought that was you. I was just telling my good friend Sara Washington—"

"Samantha," I mumbled automatically.

Scarlet scowled. "Yes, of course. Like I was saying, I was just saying that *obviously*, Clark Cunningham wasn't the intended victim. Anyone who knew him, and I certainly did know him, would know that he was such a dear man that it was obvious the killer got the wrong person." Scarlet turned up the charm, smiled, batted her eyelashes, and oozed charisma.

I eased Detective Pitt away from the mesmerizing light and camera. When we were in our corner, he finally snapped out of his hypnotic state.

"Who the devil was that?"

"That was Dr. Leonard Peters," I said. "He's a consultant for the local news. Surely, you've seen him."

Detective Pitt scowled. "This is all your fault."

I whipped my head around to face Detective Pitt. I grabbed my neck and winced. The pain stemmed from the rapid way he managed to transfer the blame for his stage fright my way. "My fault? How is this my fault?"

"These are your people—writers. Nosy. Meddling. Writers." His face was purple, although I couldn't tell if it was due to embarrassment or rage. "You're a trouble magnet. Wherever you go, there's going to be some type of trouble. If you hadn't been here, none of this would have happened."

It was obvious that Detective Pitt had concluded that I was to blame for his troubles, and no rational exposition of the facts would change his mind.

"And, if you hadn't called me, then I wouldn't be here. I

wouldn't have some Geraldo Rivera wannabe shoving a microphone in my face, trying to coerce a story out of me. You got me into this mess, and it's up to you to get me out of it."

"Wait, what?"

"You heard me, Nancy Drew. You wanna be a sleuth and solve crime, fine. Get to work."

"But I'm not trying to interfere with your investigation. In fact, I'm completely good with going home and leaving this to the professionals." I hoped a small amount of flattery would carry some weight. It didn't.

"Ha! Too late. You and the old biddies think you can get inside information that the police can't get. Go for it."

"But—"

"None of that superhero stuff. You get them to talk and then pull me in. I'm the one with the badge. I make the arrests, and I do the interviews."

"Detective Pitt, I don't—"

"I'll be close by. Don't worry." He patted his chest, indicating the place where he'd taken a bullet saving my life. "You're going to be my front person. We'll use the reporter to make the killer think he's pulled the wool over my eyes, when all the while, you'll be on the inside collecting all of the evidence." He grinned, but it looked like a grimace. "We'll show them. They can't get away with making a fool out of Bradley Pitt. No siree."

Chapter 9

"What just happened?" I turned to Frank. "As long as I've known Detective Pitt, he's ordered me to stay out of his investigations. Sure, when he was accused of murder and we helped to find the real killer, he was grateful, but . . . never has he ordered me to get involved."

Frank shrugged. "I think it's safe to say that Stinky Pitt got a bad case of stage fright and doesn't want to get caught in the spotlight of another reporter."

"He's been interviewed before . . . I think. Why this reaction? Why now? Why drag me into this?"

Frank raised an eyebrow, which spoke volumes.

"What?" I asked.

"You're here. You're an author. You belong here. Maybe he knew you would get involved regardless of whether he wanted you to or not."

I shook my head. "No. Nope. Not this time. I'm not one of them. I'm just a cozy mystery writer. I don't belong with them. I don't belong with those . . . literary artists."

"Pitt isn't the only one with imposter syndrome." Frank grabbed my shoulders and gazed into my eyes. "You do belong here. You're an author, just like everyone else here. You belong." He hugged me.

"I appreciate your totally unbiased assessment." I snuggled into his chest and could feel the laughter bubble up inside before the chuckle made its way out.

"Who said I'm unbiased? I'm completely biased in your favor." He kissed me. "That doesn't mean I'm wrong."

I pulled the ace I had up my sleeve. "I'm supposed to be planning a wedding."

"Then you'd better hurry up and get to the bottom of this murder."

Chapter 10

My cell phone vibrated, and it took a few moments for me to get it out of my purse. I wasn't surprised to see that I had several messages from Nana Jo.

Saw you and S.P. on the news

I glanced at Frank, who was reading over my shoulder. "Who's S.P.?"

"Stinky Pitt," he suggested.

He was probably right. I kept scrolling and reading.

Texted the girls and J.R.

Brunch at Franks at 10

I was able to decipher the next part. "The girls" were her friends from Shady Acres—Ruby Mae, Dorothy, and Irma. J.R. had to be my sister, Jenna Rutherford. Nana Jo assumed I would want to investigate and had gotten the ball in motion, without checking with me first. I wasn't sure if I should be flattered or angry. I peeked at Frank. "I'm sorry. She knows you don't open until eleven."

"It's fine. I can manage brunch. Besides, I've got to get my assignment too." He grinned.

I gave him a stern look, but he merely chuckled and ignored me.

Not long afterward, we were allowed to leave.

Frank drove me home and promised to have everything ready by ten tomorrow morning. I was exhausted, and he had a busy day tomorrow that was going to be starting earlier than normal, so we lingered over goodnight, parted, and went our separate ways.

Snickers and Oreo were both sound asleep when I went upstairs, and barely lifted their heads to acknowledge my arrival.

"Some watch poodles you two make," I said.

Snickers yawned and stretched.

Oreo made a few circles on the bed where he'd curled up into a ball, and then hopped down and used my leg to balance himself while stretching.

I took the poodles downstairs to take care of their business, and they made quick work of it. Before long, we were back upstairs.

Snickers took a flying leap and returned to her place on my bed.

Oreo rushed into his crate and wagged his tail. Like his ancestors before him, Oreo liked his den and considered his crate to be his safe haven. Given a choice between the wide-open spaces of my bedroom and his crate, he chose his crate every time.

I was tired, but I found sleep elusive. After tossing and turning for over an hour, I finally got up and decided to steady my nerves with a bit of writing.

Wickfield Lodge, Servants' Kitchen

"Sacked! Just like that!" Charlotte Granger snapped her fingers. She looked around the room at the faces of the Marshes' servants. Pleased with the effect, she sniffed and wiped her eyes.

Charlotte Granger was a portly middle-aged woman. Her dark hair was streaked with gray and pulled back into a severe bun at the back of her neck. Even when she wasn't crying for nearly an hour, her complexion was ruddy. Today, her eyes were as red as her cheeks.

"That's awful," Gladys said.

"Can she do that?" Flossie asked.

"Humph," Mrs. McDuffie grunted. "'Er nibs thinks she's the bloody queen of 'earts, don't she. It's 'Off with their 'eads' for all she cares."

Mrs. McDuffie, the Marshes' housekeeper, was a stout, freckle-faced woman with fluffy red hair that was thin and curly. She could be stern but had a kind heart and a firm hand.

Thompkins blanched. "Mrs. McDuffie. Please watch your language." At one time, Thompkins, the Marshes' rigidly strict butler, would have been appalled by the housekeeper's swearing, especially in front of the junior staff. However, he had learned to loosen up just the slightest bit and was genuinely fond of the housekeeper.

Flossie, the Marshes' day maid, giggled.

Mrs. Anderson, the Marshes' cook, placed a slice of seed cake on her friend's plate. "Well, if you ask

me, Lady Amelia Dallyripple doesn't deserve you."
She reached across and patted Charlotte's hand. "All
good cooks have a bit of a temper. It comes with the
territory."

Frank McTavish and Jim, the Marshes' footmen,
exchanged a glance. Mrs. Anderson was as temperamental as Charlotte.

"What's she going to do without a cook?" Millie,
the daily maid, asked.

Charlotte shrugged. "She's hired a chef from a
fancy school in Paris."

"I heard she hired a man," Gladys said.

"Wanted me to stay and assist with the day-to-day
preparations so he could focus on the fete." Charlotte
Granger grunted. "Well, I told her he could just figure
it out for himself seeing as he was so smart."

Mrs. McDuffie sipped her tea. "The nerve."

"I don't take with no foreign foods," Mrs. Anderson said, shaking her head. "Use all kinds of pecu-
liar things. Snails, octopus, and mushrooms that don't
grow right here on British soil. Why, it would serve
her right if she got poisoned eating those foreign
foods that I don't believe the Good Lord ever intended us to eat."

Thompkins bristled. "Mrs. Anderson."

"It's the truth." The Marshes' cook pursed her lips.

"If you ask me, poisoning is too good for the likes
of her," Charlotte said. She patted her friend and baking contest rival's hand. "She'll stop at nothing to get
that baking trophy away from you. Women like that
always get what's coming to them. You mark my
words. I just hope that I can be there to see her ladyship get what's coming to her."

Chapter 11

The next morning, my alarm clock went off. I opened my eyes and found myself nose to muzzle with Snickers. I smiled. Big mistake. Snickers leaned forward and licked me.

"Eww." I wiped my face.

Bigger mistake.

The moment my mouth opened, in went Snickers's tongue. After twelve years, I should have known better.

There was a knock on my door.

"Come in."

Nana Jo opened the door and stood for a few seconds watching me use my sheets to wipe the inside of my mouth. She shook her head. "How long have you had that dog? You should know better than to open your mouth when she's within licking distance."

"I think she's getting faster in her old age," I said.

Nana Jo scooped up Snickers and then walked over to the crate. The door wasn't latched, but the door had closed. She opened the door wide. "Oreo, come."

After a bit of stretching, Oreo bounded out of his crate.

"You better hurry and get dressed," Nana Jo said. "We need to meet the others at Frank's, and I have some errands to run first." She turned and walked out to let the dogs out.

It took a few minutes for Nana Jo's words to sink in. *Errands? What errands?* There was only one way to find out, so I got up and began my morning routine.

By the time I was clean and dressed, Nana Jo had brewed coffee and fed the poodles. I followed my nose to the kitchen, poured myself a large cup of the magical elixir, closed my eyes, and finished almost a full cup in one long, slow slurp. The caffeine flowed through my body. Nana Jo knew me well enough to know talking would be better after I had downed at least one full cup of coffee.

"Are you human yet?"

"Just about." I sipped my coffee. "What errands?"

"You need to swing by the police station and talk to Detective Pitt."

I started to protest, but Nana Jo held up a hand to stop me. "We both know Stinky Pitt isn't going to want anyone to know you're doing the real work solving murders while he sits back and takes all of the credit. So, if you want any of the insider information, you're going to need to go to him."

"Insider information?"

She waved her hand. "Forensics, medical examiner stuff. You know what I mean."

"Okay, I noticed you said *I* need to go to him. Aren't you coming?"

"No, I want you to drop me off at North Harbor Hospital. I have a friend who works there. I'm going to pump her like a bicycle tire to find out what she knows about Clark Cunningham's death. The hospital isn't far from the police station, and I should be done well before you finish with Stinky Pitt."

Wow. I had been awake for less than an hour and Nana Jo had already organized my morning. I wasn't complaining. I needed her organizational skills.

After a few minutes of pacing expectantly, the poodles had given up on the possibility of snagging anything to eat and were lying at my feet. Suddenly, they sat up. Oreo cocked his head to the side and listened. Snickers was older, and I suspected her hearing wasn't as good as it had once been. Although, she could still hear a food wrapper being opened from a solid fifty yards away. After a moment, they both got up and hurried downstairs, and I could hear footsteps and the sound of toenails clicking on the hardwood.

Dawson Alexander was one of the few people who had a key. Besides, the barking was playful, so even before I saw Dawson's head pop up over the railing, I knew that whoever was ascending was a friend and not a dangerous criminal with evil intentions. Although, given the fact that my grandmother was a crack shot and a black belt in aikido, I pitied the fool who would try to break in and confront my nana.

"Good morning," Dawson said. "I wanted to try out a new recipe if that's okay."

"Only if you leave plenty for us to try," Nana Jo joked.

Dawson knew the rules. He placed a grocery bag on the counter. Since his baking benefitted the patrons of the bookstore, I reimbursed him for any ingredients he bought on his own.

To say that Dawson grew up poor would have been a big understatement. His mother left when he was a baby, and he'd been raised by an abusive alcoholic father. His football scholarship was his ticket to a better life, and he intended to make the most of it. When my mother recently remarried, her husband, Harold Robertson, was not only extremely kind and devoted to my mother, he was also as wealthy as Midas. Before setting off to Australia to save the koala bears, Harold had given each of my nephews a hefty trust fund. Leon and I never had children of our own, but Dawson was the child I'd never had, and Harold left a tidy sum for him too. Initially, I had worried that Dawson would go on a spending spree and blow all of his money on expensive clothes, fast cars, and even faster women. However, living in poverty convinced him that he never wanted to be poor again. Dawson had invested his money.

Nana Jo and I left Dawson baking and the poodles circling the floor in the hopes that he would drop something delicious. The floor was their territory, and anything that hit it was fair game.

North Harbor Hospital was only a short distance from the police station. I dropped Nana Jo at the hospital's main entrance and then headed back across the St. Thomas bridge toward downtown. North Harbor and its twin city of South Harbor shared the same Lake Michigan coastline, but the two cities couldn't be more different. North Harbor was economically depressed, while South Harbor was a postcard-perfect resort town. Both towns were separated by the St. Thomas River, which zigzagged through northern Indiana and southern Michigan for over two hundred miles, wrapped around North Harbor in a U, and flowed into Lake Michigan. The police station was in a brick two-story building near both the lake and river.

Locals referred to the police station as the North Harbor Police Station, although the name had changed decades ago. The police station now serviced the entire county and was attached to the county courthouse. The combined buildings created a sprawling complex situated on a small street between both cities.

Inside, I placed my purse and shoes on a conveyor belt and

went through a metal detector that rivaled that of the River Bend airport. Bad memories of an incident where Nana Jo forgot to remove her Peacemaker from her purse meant that I held my breath until I was safely through to the other side.

Once I was inside, I went to the main desk and asked for Detective Pitt. I didn't have to wait long.

Detective Pitt came to the front, scowled, and then motioned me to follow him.

I trailed him through the maze of cubicles and perimeter offices back to the closet he called an office. In actuality, my closet at home was larger than his office. Detective Pitt used the hooks on the wall, which used to hold brooms, to hang his jacket.

In order to close the door, I had to squeeze closer to the desk, close the fold-up chair he used as a desk chair, and hold it to my body. Once the door was closed, Detective Pitt and I maneuvered around each other like square dancers. He scooted around me to sit behind his desk, while I opened the folding chair and sat.

"Alright, what do you want?" he asked.

What do I want? I want to go home and mind my own business. Deep breaths. "You asked me to help figure out who murdered Clark Cunningham. I didn't think you would want to be seen talking to me at MISU, so I came—"

"Alright. Never mind." He waved his hand as though swatting away a fly.

I forced my brow to unfurl. My lips refused to lift beyond neutral, but that was good enough. I waited.

Detective Pitt's desk looked as though a file cabinet had exploded, and it was covered in an avalanche of file folders, papers, and fast-food wrappers. He picked up a glazed donut, which was teetering on a mountain of papers, and crammed it into his mouth. Detective Pitt was talented. He multitasked by eating a donut, licking glaze from his fingers, and hunting down the file he was looking for. Only a few crumbs of hardened glaze escaped his mouth, landing on his shirt and the folders on his desk. He cleaned himself up by wetting his finger and tapping the crumbs. He did all of this without losing focus. He ate. He cleaned. He rifled through papers, eventually found what he was looking for, and passed me the folder.

I wasn't a germophobe, but it took quite a bit of effort to touch that folder without grimacing. Having worked as a high school teacher, my tolerance for the gross and disgusting was fairly high. Still, it took all of my mental energy to avoid wiping my hands on my jeans.

Balancing the folder on my lap, I opened it and read. There wasn't much. The preliminary cause of death was likely due to cyanide poisoning, but it wasn't confirmed. They wouldn't know more until the autopsy was completed. I flipped through the folder looking for more. When I didn't see anything, I turned to Detective Pitt. "Is this all you've got?"

He had shoved another donut into his mouth and didn't bother to finish chewing before responding. "Mats mall."

"Excuse me?"

He swallowed and slurped coffee. "That's all, but we're holding back that the poison was cyanide."

"Did you get anything from the statements?"

"Nothing worth investigating." He flipped through some papers on his desk and pulled up a telephone memo. He scanned it. "That dingbat aura lady thinks she saw a vision of the waiter who gave Cunningham the poisoned champagne while meditating this morning. She feels certain she could identify him again." He crushed the message into a ball and tossed it in the general direction of the trash can. The trash can was overflowing, so the wadded message bounced off the stack and onto the floor.

"Great." I placed the folder on the edge of his desk and stood. "Well, I'm going to pick up Nana Jo and meet with the group at Frank's, and then I'm heading for campus." I folded my chair and prepared to leave.

"Hold on. Not so fast." Detective Pitt motioned for me to sit down.

I unfolded my chair and complied. Once seated, I stared at Detective Pitt.

"The M.E. may not have anything yet, but I ran some of these names through our system." He grinned and stared as though he was waiting for applause.

"Great. What did you find?"

"I really wanted to get something on that so-called reporter." He sucked his teeth and shook his head. After a few moments, he shook his head again.

"I take it you didn't find anything on *Dr.* Leonard Peters." I couldn't stop myself from emphasizing the *doctor.*

"Humph! That's another thing. He's not a *real* doctor. Just some lawyer with a string of letters after his name."

I should have known my sarcasm would be lost on Stinky Pitt. I was tempted to explain that a PhD was just a different type of doctor, but I would be wasting my breath. Instead, I asked, "What did you find?"

"That fella that was drunk, Paul West, has gotten a couple of DUIs."

"That's scary. I hope his wife drove."

"Well, he didn't get arrested last night at any rate." He glanced at his printout. "That crazy aura lady threatened Judith Hunter at some event in New York a few months back.

When Clark Cunningham tried to intervene and break it up, he nearly got his eyes clawed out."

"Who did the clawing?" I had a feeling I already knew the answer, but I asked the question anyway.

"Nora Cooper."

That's what I thought.

"So, while she *says* no one would want to kill Clark Cunningham, it sounds like she may be trying to direct suspicion away from herself."

I didn't believe Nora Cooper was capable of that much deception, but what did I know? I'd only met the woman yesterday. Geez! Had it only been one day?

He didn't have much. Everyone else was clean, at least as far as the police were concerned. He promised to track me down on campus later, after he cleaned up a few files.

I hoped he meant literally, but I knew better.

Leaving the police station was a lot easier than arriving. I made it to my car and pulled away from the curb with no incidents.

Nana Jo was waiting when I picked her up a few minutes later. I drove home and parked in the garage, and we walked the short distance to Frank's restaurant. Parking on the street downtown was never easy, even before the lunchtime rush. Plus, I hated taking a parking space away from any of Frank's customers. The food was so good, most people were willing to park farther away and walk, but there was no reason when I had a perfectly good garage nearby. And the walk was good exercise. It gave me time to think about Detective Pitt's argument that Nora Cooper may have deliberately killed Clark Cunningham while feigning a false personality. It seemed farfetched at first, but I couldn't eliminate it completely. A creative type like an author just might try to deflect suspicion away from herself by pretending to be a bit . . . scatty in order to throw the police off her trail. We walked to Frank's while I mulled over the possibilities. However, I was left with a lot of questions and no answers. First, was everything Nora Cooper did just an act? Was she really plotting to kill Clark Cunningham all along and only pretending that Judith Hunter was her enemy? Was Nora Cooper really as odd as she came across? Or was she faking? Was Nora Cooper smart enough or deceptive enough to pull this off? And lastly, why would she want to kill Clark Cunningham?

Chapter 12

It was early, and technically, Frank's place wasn't open for business yet, so we had our choice of tables. However, we'd grown accustomed to meeting upstairs where we would be out of the way of the servers and away from the general restaurant crowd. So, when the hostess let us in, we weren't surprised when she headed upstairs.

Similar to most of the buildings on our block, the restaurant had a business on the first floor at street level. Over time, many of the area's brownstone owners had converted the upstairs to apartments that were rented out for additional income. Frank's upstairs had never been converted into living space. Instead, it was a large, open area that he planned to use for private parties. So far, our group were the only ones who used the space. It needed to be spruced up, but he wasn't ready to tackle that job just yet. He was still upgrading the building's older infrastructure, running his restaurant, and planning a wedding. Upstairs renovations would likely require closing down the lower level, so it was set on the back burner. Our group didn't mind in the least.

When we got upstairs, Dorothy, Irma, Ruby Mae, and Jenna were already seated and drinking coffee. In Jenna's case, there was a small pot of tea, which I knew without looking contained her favorite—Royal English Breakfast.

I sat next to my sister, but one glance told me that she wasn't fully caffeinated yet. So, when I said, "Good morning," and she merely grunted, I didn't take it personally.

I poured myself a cup of coffee and added cream and artificial sweetener. One of the things that made Frank such a great host was that he remembered what people liked, including Jenna's favorite drink; my favorite sweetener—the blue packages; and Nana Jo's favorite orange juice—freshly squeezed but strained to remove all pulp. And it wasn't just my family's favorites he remembered. He had an excellent memory, especially for people who came to the restaurant regularly, and he catered to them.

Not long after we arrived, our server, Morgan, brought up a tray filled with pastries. She was followed by two waiters carrying chafing dishes with bacon and eggs.

When Morgan had dropped off her platter, she came by and gave me a hug. Last week, Morgan's hair had been dyed purple. Today, it was teal. One side was shaved. But instead of the normal spiked mohawk, she wore it down in a bob.

"I love the teal," I said.

Morgan beamed. "Thanks. I got bored, so . . ."

"Any new tattoos?"

Morgan had a tattoo sleeve that depicted characters from the Chronicles of Narnia. The rest of her body was covered in tattoos that reflected her other interests, including an orange Tigger from *Winnie-the-Pooh* on her shoulder. She shook her head. "Not yet. I had the perfect tattoo picked out. It was a heart and flag, but my brother said it would be disrespectful to have the flag on my butt because I would be sitting on it. It's not like anyone would see it." She shrugged and then hurried downstairs.

Nana Jo was sitting next to me at the head of the table. She leaned close and said, "You tell that girl she doesn't have to worry about sitting on the flag. Her biggest problem is gravity."

I tilted my head to the side and stared at my grandmother. "What do you mean?"

"By the time she's my age, nature and gravity will be her biggest problems. That's when she'll experience the great shift. That tattoo on her butt will have dropped down to her thighs."

Jenna leaned closer to me and said, "Makes you wonder how she knows so much about this, doesn't it?"

Nana Jo tapped her spoon on a glass to get everyone's attention. "Okay, let's get this party started. Sam has to get over to the college, and Frank will be busy with the lunch crowd."

Frank chose that moment to come upstairs. He carried a pitcher of water with lemons. My favorite. He was such a thoughtful man. Jenna got up to move so that Frank could sit next to me, but he stopped her. "I can't stay. I have a lot to do downstairs. I just wanted to make sure everyone had what they needed."

Everyone was good and let Frank know how much they appreciated the food.

He poured a glass of lemon water for me, placed the pitcher in front of me, and then gave me a kiss. He whispered, "I'll see you later tonight to get my assignment." Frank's work in the military had been top secret, but he'd made connections that enabled him to gain access to information the rest of us never could get.

I watched him hurry downstairs and thought about how incredibly blessed I was to have found love again after my late husband Leon's death.

"Earth to Sam," Nana Jo said.

"Sorry, what did you say?"

"I asked if you wanted to tell us what happened last night, who the primary suspects were, and anything you learned from Stinky Pitt this morning." Nana Jo pulled her iPad from her purse and prepared to take notes.

I quickly gave everyone a recap of all of the events, including the fact that the general consensus was that Clark Cunningham wasn't the primary target.

"Sounds like Judith Hunter was the intended victim," Ruby Mae said.

"Especially since you said Clark Cunningham spilled his drink and Judith Hunter gave him hers," Dorothy said.

Nana Jo narrowed her gaze. "Do you have doubts?"

"No," I said. "It's just something Detective Pitt said this morning." I shared the detective's theory that Nora Cooper may have deliberately wanted to make it seem as though Judith Hunter was the intended victim, when in actuality she really had it out for Clark Cunningham all along.

"I don't know how much stock I'd put in a theory that Stinky Pitt came up with," Nana Jo said. "His track record hasn't been the greatest."

Nana Jo had a point. In the past, Detective Pitt had accused me, Nana Jo, my stepfather Harold Robertson, and my assistant Dawson Alexander of murder. "That's true, but I suppose there's always a first time . . ."

"It's worth investigating. You know what they say, 'Even a broke clock is right twice each day.'" Nana Jo told the others about her trip to the hospital. "I didn't find out much at the hospital this morning. My friend is a nurse and she was working last night. She said Clark Cunningham was dead by the time the EMTs arrived at the hospital. The doctors took blood samples, but that's all she could tell me." Nana Jo bit her lip.

"What's bothering you?" I asked.

"It's just something she mentioned. Apparently, Judith Hunter arrived at the hospital not long after Clark Cunningham was brought in. She claimed to be family. When the staff told her he was dead, she demanded his personal belongings."

"What belongings?" I said. "He was at a fancy dinner. It's not like he had a briefcase or laptop."

"Exactly. She wanted his wallet, clothes, and cell phone."

"Maybe she was afraid someone would steal it," Ruby Mae said. "Whenever I've had to go to the hospital, I always make sure my family has my purse and belongings. I'm not saying the hospital staff steal, but there's always so many people coming and going that sometimes things can get lost in a hospital."

"Apparently, Judith made a fuss and threatened to sue the hospital," Nana Jo said.

"Did they give it to her?" I asked.

Nana Jo shook her head. "Nope. If he had been alive, they would have, but he was dead."

"Grief can make people act strange," Dorothy said.

"I know, but just when they were about to bag his personal items for her, they got the call from Stinky Pitt to treat it as a homicide, so they couldn't release anything. That's when she became hysterical. She started bawling like a baby."

"Shock?" I asked.

"My friend said she thought they were going to need to strap her down and shoot her up with tranquilizers to settle her down, but then she pulled herself together. She said she was fine. She refused treatment and ran out of the hospital." Nana Jo looked down her nose at each of us. "Now that looks suspicious."

"It does look suspicious," I said. "But . . . I don't know how I'd respond if someone I knew suddenly died and the police thought it was murder."

"Especially if it finally dawned on her that maybe the poison that killed Clark Cunningham was meant for her," Jenna said.

We pondered Judith's odd behavior for several moments. When we'd gone in circles enough times, we decided that maybe we needed to investigate Judith and her relationship with Clark Cunningham. Were they so close that she considered herself family? Or were they more than family?

Nana Jo turned to me. "Now, what are our assignments?"

"Our most likely suspects would be Nora Cooper, Scarlet MacDunkin, Paul West, and Olivia Townsend. But I think we should also look into Clark Cunningham, Mrs. Graves, and Leonard Peters. I don't know that they had a reason to kill Clark Cunningham or Judith Hunter, but it doesn't hurt to eliminate them from the list." I turned to Nana Jo. "Anyway, I invited Paul West to the store to sign stock, so if he shows up, maybe you can talk to him."

"Got it," Nana Jo said. "Plus, I'll ask Freddie to have his son, Mark, see if he can dig anything up on any of the people involved."

Freddie Williams was Nana Jo's boyfriend, and his son Mark was a Michigan State Police officer. He often ran some of our suspects through the police database and provided information, especially when Detective Pitt was trying to exclude us from his investigations.

Ruby Mae finished eating and pulled out her knitting. Today, she was making a pale blue baby blanket. Her great-granddaughter was expecting a baby around Christmas, and Ruby Mae had shifted into baby prep mode. "My cousin's grandson works in the MISU library, so I can talk to him. He might know something about Mrs. Graves. I think he mentioned that she was a dean or assistant dean and somehow connected to the library."

"Great," I said. "I don't think she poisoned Clark Cunningham or anyone, but it wouldn't hurt to hear if he's heard anything that might be helpful." I wasn't sure where I was going with that. Neither Graves nor Peters were anywhere near Judith Hunter, that I could see. Still, something was nagging at my brain.

"I'd like to tackle Leonard Peters," Irma said. "He's a hunk."

Nana Jo rolled her eyes. Irma was man-crazy, but she often got results.

"Are you still . . . ah . . . friendly with that professor?" I asked.

Irma patted her hair. "I'm friendly with a lot of people."

"Smith . . . Professor Smith. I think you were, um . . . dating him when Detective Pitt was accused of murdering that politician, John Cloverton."

"Oh, Smithy . . . yeah, we went out several times, but then I moved on. I suppose I could give him a call." Irma glanced at me in a way that made me think she was making a huge sacrifice.

"If it wouldn't be too much trouble," I said.

Irma took out a compact and checked her makeup. "I'm always willing to take one for the team." She giggled.

"Ugh," Nana Jo said. "Let's move on before I lose my breakfast."

"Dorothy, doesn't one of your grandsons own a magazine?" I asked.

"Actually, it's my great-nephew. He's Jillian's cousin, Jacob Friedman. Why do you ask?"

"And weren't you a journalism major in college?"

"Yes, back when dinosaurs roamed the earth, but yes. I majored in journalism at Northwestern University and then worked for several magazines before I got married and settled down to domestic life."

"I was thinking maybe your nephew might consider hiring you to do a little freelance journalism for his magazine. Perhaps you could do a story on Judith Hunter and the book festival. That would give you an excuse to hang around the book festival, but more importantly, to hang around Judith Hunter."

"Okay, but it's been decades since I've done any actual reporting. However, something makes me think there's more to this request than you're saying."

"Actually, I'm concerned that if Judith Hunter was the real intended victim, the killer might try again. If Detective Pitt really believes that Clark Cunningham was the killer's target, he might not take sufficient precautions to make sure that the killer doesn't make another attempt. Besides, you would be a lot less obvious than a policeman standing around. And you could be her bodyguard."

The idea of a seventy-year-old woman as a bodyguard may have seemed strange, but anyone who knew Dorothy Clark knew that not only was she nearly six feet tall, but she also had a black belt in aikido and was well on her way to a black belt in judo too.

"Sure, I can do that. Maybe I can follow her around and say I want to get a feel for a day in her life or something like that. I can call Jacob and give him a heads-up in case she decides to check my story."

I glanced around the table. Everyone had their assignments except my sister. She didn't look as though she would mind skipping this round, but it never hurts to have a lawyer on your side. "Jenna, I'm almost ninety-nine percent sure that Leonard Peters didn't have anything to do with murdering Clark Cunningham, but I was hoping you could reach out to your legal friends and see if there's any reason why he would want to kill Clark Cunningham or Judith Hunter."

"Is that all?"

"Well, if you could look up the law around plagiarism, that would be great." I could see Jenna revving up. She had told me many times since I got my first contract that her specialty was criminal law and that she was not a contract specialist. I decided to preempt the lecture. "I know publishing contracts aren't your thing, but how long would Judith get if she were found guilty of plagiarism?"

"Nothing."

"What do you mean, nothing?"

"Nothing. Plagiarism isn't a crime."

"WHAT!" everyone said.

"Plagiarism is unethical and *might* be illegal if the plagiarized work was published and had a copyright. In that case, copyright infringement is illegal and could be costly."

"Wow," I said. "That doesn't seem fair."

"Justice and fairness aren't the same thing. The law is supposed to be just and impartial. It isn't necessarily fair."

"So, it's okay for Judith Hunter to steal Nora's book and nothing would happen?" Nana Jo asked.

Jenna shook her head. "That's not what I'm saying. The question was whether plagiarism is a crime. The answer is no. However, it sounds like what Nora Cooper was accusing Judith Hunter of was actually theft, which is a crime. I need to do some research. The legal question becomes if Judith stole the material from Nora and made a ton of money, then it could make it a felony." Jenna sipped her tea. "However, when she stole the manuscript, what was its value? I'd need to do some research."

"I'll talk to my agent too and find out what it would mean for her career, but I suspect I already know the answer to that one."

"Great," Nana Jo said. "Everyone has their assignments. What are you going to do?"

I glanced at my phone for the time. "I have a panel discussion in thirty minutes. Then, I'm going to call my publicist, Larissa Addo, to find out what she knows about Clark Cunningham, Judith Hunter, and the others. She's always telling me that publishing is a small world. It's time for me to find out exactly how small."

Chapter 13

On my way out, I stopped by the kitchen to say goodbye to Frank. He was elbow deep in a large bowl of potato salad. So, I merely asked if he could ask a friend to find out about Judith Hunter's and Nora Cooper's financial situations. If Nora Cooper was telling the truth, maybe he could see if Judith paid someone a large sum of money. I mean, surely no one would take someone else's work for nothing.

Frank promised to check into it.

Nana Jo and I walked back to the store. She went inside to get things ready for the day, while I hurried to my car and headed back to campus.

It took a few trips around the visitor lot before I found a parking space, and I had to run to make it in time for my panel, but I made it.

When I first started my book tour, I didn't realize that authors often participated on more than one panel. However, I'd learned that the number of panels an author did depended a great deal on the number of authors participating. Multiple panels meant more exposure, so while it could be tiring, it was great, especially for a new author. My publicist had gotten me on three. Today's panel discussion was a lot more low-key than the one yesterday with Judith Hunter and Scarlet Mac-Dunkin. Although, the turnout was definitely bigger. Today's panel featured me and a woman named Kitty Carlson. Kitty was an environmentalist who had written a romance novel that combined her passion for the planet with her passion for . . . well, passionate books. Her protagonist was an environmental activist who falls in love with the CEO of a manufacturing plant that is polluting the water and air in a small town in Pennsylvania. By the end of the book, not only does the love of a good woman convince him to change his ways, but he commits his life to protecting the planet and the woman he loves. It was a touching story. Plus, she was using her talent to promote sustainability. Not only was her book impressive, but she was wearing an outfit made completely from plastic bags. I learned that eight million tons of plastic are dumped in the ocean every year. Kitty challenged me and everyone in the audience to use our platforms to make a difference and save the planet.

She got a standing ovation.

I talked about the inspiration for my British historic cozy mystery series. I did not get a standing ovation. Just when I was getting over my feelings of inferiority . . . here I was again. And to make matters worse, her plastic bag dress looked pretty amazing. Of course, when you're a size two, you can look good wearing just about anything, even plastic bags. Sigh.

Afterward, I walked down the crowded hallway. The number of people today was more than double that of those who attended the opening-day events, so it took longer. Any concerns over a murder causing people to avoid the book festival were put to rest. Curiosity seekers showed up in droves. There were news trucks and reporters interviewing authors and fans. Nothing like a murder to bring out attention seekers.

Eventually, I made my way through the crowd and turned the corner to my table. Today, I was grateful to be out of the limelight and away from the hordes. Why would anyone want to talk to me anyway? My characters weren't saving the environment. My cozy mystery *was* set in Great Britain at the start of World War II, so technically they would need to save the world from evil. Maybe I could have Lady Elizabeth talk about the evils of plastic bags. *Did they have plastic bags in Great Britain in 1939?* I made a mental note to check.

I shelved the guilt for not writing environment-saving books right next to the guilt I felt for not writing books that saved the rainforest or the Amur leopard. If I wasn't careful, my shelves would be overflowing with guilt. Alright, overflowing even more than they were already.

I checked the time and decided that I needed to get busy. With any luck, I could figure out who killed Clark Cunningham and get home before I found myself buried under more guilt. I called my agent, Pamela Porter.

"Hey, Sam! I was just thinking about you. Is it true? Did someone murder Clark Cunningham at the North Harbor Book Festival?"

"How'd you hear about that already?"

"Wow! So, it is true."

"Sadly, yes. In fact, I was wondering what you could tell me about him or Judith Hunter."

"Aww. So, that's true too. I had heard that whoever killed Clark was aiming for Judith. Actually, that makes more sense."

"Oh? Spill it. What do you know?"

Pamela Porter was a tough-as-nails Black woman who had spent twenty years in publishing before opening her own boutique agency. It took a while for me to understand the lingo, but *boutique* seemed to mean she had a one-woman agency. I trusted her and valued her insight. The fact that she was running a successful agency alone was a testament to her strength, determination, and resilience. She was a dynamo, and I was lucky to have her representing me.

She pounded on the keys of her laptop. "Well, if you're at the North Harbor Book Festival with both Judith Hunter and Nora Cooper, I'm sure you've heard the dirt. Nora tells everyone who will listen that she wrote *The Corpse Danced at Midnight* and Judith Hunter stole it."

"Do you believe her?"

Pamela paused. "I don't know. It's different from Judith's other books. Very different, but it's a different style of book too."

"Is it Nora's style?"

"Honestly, it doesn't read like either one of them. It's well written and taps into feelings that neither author had shown in previous books."

Pamela was holding something back.

"What aren't you telling me?"

She paused for several beats. "It's just odd. If you're going to take a big risk, wouldn't you want a sure thing?"

"I guess so."

"Look, if I'm going to risk the possibility of jail for stealing, it's not going to be some chump change little five-and-dime. If I'm going to take that type of risk, then you better believe I've figured out a way to break into Fort Knox. Nora Cooper isn't a brilliant writer. So, if you're Judith Hunter and willing to risk your reputation and possibly jail by stealing a manuscript and peddling it off as your own, why not steal a sure thing? Break into Stephen King's laptop. Nora Cooper isn't well-known enough to guarantee that the manuscript will be a success, no matter how well written it is. There are tens of thousands of good, really good manuscripts printed every year. Yet, even with a good manuscript, there's no guarantee that it'll sell more than a handful of books."

"I never thought of that before."

"I don't know Judith or Nora personally. I can't say if it's in their characters to cheat, but I just don't buy it."

"So, you think Judith really did write the book?" I asked.

"I honestly don't know."

"Publicity?"

"Maybe. It's not the type of publicity I would want for any of my clients, but I suppose it's possible. Anything's possible."

Pamela and I didn't chat long. She was a busy woman, and I knew she had probably been up since five thirty in the morning, so I cut it short and let her get back to work.

I sat for several minutes thinking about what Pamela said long after I'd hung up the phone. Stealing the manuscript would be risky. I didn't know Judith well enough to know if she was the type of person who liked taking risks, but maybe I could find out.

The crowds in the main hallway were loud, and I found myself distracted. Sadly, my distraction was due to the noise, not to people. Few people turned the corner to come near my table unless they were heading to the restroom. I took out my laptop. Maybe spending some time in 1939 would help inspire me.

Wickfield Lodge, Study

Lady Elizabeth stood at the window of the study and looked out onto the lawn as a small army of workers toted tables, strung lights and banners, and prepared tents for the fete. Hearing a slight cough, Lady Elizabeth turned to see her butler, Thompkins.

"Lord James FitzAndrew Browning, the Fifteenth Duke of Kingfordshire," Thompkins announced.

Lord Browning entered the room, walked over to Lady Elizabeth, and kissed her cheek. "What's with Thompkins? I didn't think it was possible for him to become more proper, but I think he has."

"Ever since he returned from Windsor Castle, he's been drilling all of the staff on proper etiquette and decorum." Lady Elizabeth smiled. "What a pleasant surprise." She glanced around. "Is Daphne with you?"

"No, her doctor has ordered her to bed rest, or nothing would have prevented her from coming to spend time with her family."

"Is she okay?"

Lord Browning reassured her that both Lady Daphne and the heir to the dukedom were well.

"Wonderful. I can't wait to see her and, of course, the baby. We're coming in a few weeks. Anyway, let's have tea, and you can fill me in on all of the preparations." She walked to the wall by the fireplace and pushed a small button. Then she took a seat on the sofa and waited for Lord Browning to join her.

Before Lady Elizabeth could request tea, Thompkins reappeared, pushing a cart.

"Thompkins, you are wonderful," she said. "I think you're learning to read my mind."

Only a close observer would have noticed the sparkle in the butler's eye or the slight tinge of pink that crept above his starched white collar. He bowed stiffly and then turned and left.

Lady Elizabeth poured tea for her nephew. He helped himself to a scone from the platter of goodies the cook had prepared.

Lord Browning told Lady Elizabeth every detail

that his wife, Lady Elizabeth's niece, Daphne, was preparing in anticipation of their first baby. She'd decorated the nursery first in bright yellow, but then she changed her mind and redecorated in mint green before returning to the original yellow. "She's interviewed at least a hundred nannies." He shook his head, but there was a twinkle in his eye.

"And I'm guessing that the baby's father has perhaps used his connections to investigate these same nannies." Lady Elizabeth gave the duke a meaningful glance.

"I might have checked out a few of the top contenders." He chuckled.

The two spent several minutes talking about all things baby until they had finished their tea.

"William's gone to his club in London to escape all of the preparations for the village fete," Lady Elizabeth said. "He'll be sorry he missed you, but he'll be back later tonight." She set her teacup on the tray and pulled out her knitting from the bag she kept near the sofa. "Although, I suspect you already know that," she said shrewdly.

"I can't sneak anything past you, can I?" His admiration and respect for Lady Elizabeth had grown significantly since he'd first met her. She'd proven to be trustworthy and of keen mind, which was why he was here. "What can you tell me about Colonel Basil Livingston?"

Lady Elizabeth paused for a brief moment. "Not much. I've never met the man, although he's supposed to be doing a book reading at Lady Dallyripple's tonight." She glanced at the duke. "However, I suspect you already know that too."

"You're right. I am here unofficially on *official* business. Colonel Basil Livingston is a person of interest in intelligence circles at the moment."

"So he really is a colonel?"

"Yes. He distinguished himself in the Great War. He settled down in a small village not far from here. He wrote a not very well-received book about his time in the military. However, we've received intel that he is now working on a new book, which he claims will be a tell-all look inside the British military."

"Can he do that?" Lady Elizabeth asked.

"We don't know."

"Did he have access to information that might be damaging to the military?"

"Again, we don't know."

"But it's been more than twenty years since the end of the war. Surely, nothing he might have been privy to at that time would still be relevant today." Lady Elizabeth frowned. "It just seems that everything is so advanced now."

"You'd be amazed at how many things haven't changed. But, therein lies the dilemma, and given our current state of affairs with Germany, we just can't take the chance that anything of importance could leak out." He stood and paced. "Most people don't take his claims seriously. They think he's just trying to play on the public's fears of the impending war to chalk up publicity for his book. However, there are some within the government who are concerned."

"So, you're here to find out what he knows?" Lady Elizabeth asked.

"It would be more convincing if I could have

brought Daphne with me. Then my visit would simply be chalked up to Lady Daphne Browning coming home to Wickfield Lodge to spend time with her family before her confinement. Nothing suspicious."

Lady Elizabeth smiled. "As opposed to MI5 taking a special interest in the happenings at a village fete?"

"Exactly."

Lady Elizabeth was one of a short list of individuals who actually knew about the duke's secret career as a member of Britain's secret intelligence organization.

"Well, I'm disappointed that Daphne wasn't able to come with you, but she needs plenty of rest in her condition." Lady Elizabeth continued to knit before asking, "What can you tell me about Colonel Livingston?"

"He wasn't particularly well liked. He thought he knew more than everyone else, but that's not a crime."

"Did he have access to sensitive information?"

Lord Browning hesitated a moment. "He might have. Colonel Livingston's rise through the ranks was largely due to his connections. One of those connections was a general with a partiality for loose women, Cuban cigars, and malt whiskey. I'm afraid he wasn't known for discretion, and when he'd had too much of any of his vices, he tended to run off at the mouth."

"Oh, dear me. Surely, this general is a liability. The government should do something about him."

"The general had connections too. He was moved to a small outpost in Bermuda. We believed if he talked there, it wouldn't matter." Lord Browning crossed one leg over the other and leaned back. "However, we have reason to believe Livingston traveled to Bermuda to meet with the general. When

Livingston returned, that's when he started talking about this new book."

"What about the general?"

"He had an accident. We believe he was a victim of a robbery gone bad."

Lady Elizabeth gazed at her nephew. She wondered if the general's death really was a mistake or whether he might have been helped into the afterlife.

"We discovered some classified documents in his possession. Documents that should never have left the War Office. If Livingston got hold of those, then . . ." He shook his head.

"Couldn't someone just ask him?"

"We tried, but he refused to say. He has his rights, and he won't be censored." Lord Browning rose and paced in front of the fireplace. "If we knew for sure what information he'd gotten hold of, then we would know our next steps. That's where you come in."

Lady Elizabeth stopped knitting and gave her nephew her full, undivided attention.

"I need you to keep Colonel Livingston here while I search through his belongings." Lord Browning turned to glance at his aunt for a sign that would indicate the direction she would take. Lady Elizabeth Marsh was an intelligent woman, but she also had a high moral standard. Would she agree to be a party to a deliberate illegal act? Of that, he wasn't sure.

Lady Elizabeth picked up her knitting. Before she could respond, the study doors were opened, and Thompkins stood stiff and proper.

"I beg your ladyship's pardon, but Lady Dallyripple is—" Before Thompkins could explain, Lady Dallyripple pushed through the door.

"Elizabeth, the most horrible catastrophe has be-fallen me. You absolutely *must* help me." Lady Dally-ripple marched in and flopped down on the sofa.

Lady Elizabeth locked eyes with the butler. After a slight inclination of her head toward the tea cart, he nodded and backed out of the room, closing the doors behind him.

"Lord James Browning, Lady Amelia Dallyripple. Amelia, you remember Lord Browning is Daphne's husband." Lady Elizabeth completed the introduc-tions, sat back on the sofa, and pulled out her knitting. She paused for a few moments before continuing. "Now, Amelia. What's the catastrophe?"

Thompkins entered and quietly exchanged the tea cart with one laden with another tiered platter of sandwiches, delectable goodies, and a fresh pot of tea.

Lady Elizabeth smiled to herself. She couldn't help but suspect that this elaborate display was meant to impress Lady Dallyripple and was perhaps her cook, Mrs. Anderson, throwing down the gaunt-let regarding the upcoming baking competition.

Lady Dallyripple accepted the teacup and plate. "Thank you, Elizabeth. I have to admit, I'm famished. I've been working my fingers to the bone and didn't have time to eat more than a meager breakfast and a few sandwiches for lunch." She sipped the tea and quickly devoured three sandwich triangles. "It's a wonder I haven't collapsed."

Having seen Lady Dallyripple's idea of what con-stituted a "meager breakfast," Lady Elizabeth wasn't concerned that her neighbor was in any physical jeopardy. She waited while her guest finished off a scone and put down her teacup.

"It's just awful. Water everywhere. Everything's

ruined. And the servants are up in arms about Charlotte. Of course, they won't say anything to me, but I'm sure one of them is behind this mess. Why, there's just no way my precious Phoebe or Clara could have caused that much damage. I'm being sabotaged. There's just no other explanation."

Lord Browning frowned and glanced at Elizabeth, who shook her head.

"Amelia, I understand you're upset," Lady Elizabeth said, "but you're just going to need to stop and take a deep breath and tell us what happened."

"That's what I'm doing," Lady Amelia huffed. "It's the electrical. It's not working. Bradford has accused Phoebe and Clara of chewing the cords. If he wasn't such a good butler whose family has served the Dallyripples for millennia, I would have sacked him right then and there. How dare he blame those two innocent girls."

Lady Elizabeth shared a knowing glance with Lord Browning. "Phoebe and Clara are two of Amelia's corgis."

"And those two precious babies would never do anything of the kind," Lady Amelia said. She took a sip from her newly refilled teacup before continuing. "They were playing in the room when that dull-witted girl, Louise, came in with the flowers. She *claims* they deliberately tripped her, and she dropped the vase, getting water on everything. And that vase was a wedding present from my great-aunt Margaret. I'm sure it cost a small fortune because the box came from Lalique, and I know she bought it when she was in Paris." She stood up and paced from the sofa to the fireplace, only stopping to get another watercress sandwich. "Have you ever heard anything so ridiculous? Alfred doesn't care. He said the vase was hideous, and he never cared for it one bit. But that's not the point. I believe that girl deliberately destroyed that valuable vase to get back at me for sacking Charlotte Granger. Well, I'll make sure she—"

"Amelia," Lady Elizabeth said, "I'm sure Louise wouldn't deliberately destroy an expensive vase simply out of spite, but that's neither here nor there. Having a valuable vase destroyed is disappointing, but it can hardly be classified as catastrophic. Now, please tell us calmly and rationally what happened."

"I'm always calm and rational." Lady Amelia frowned. "When that silly girl doused those wires with the water from the vase, it caused problems with the electric. Lionel Cuthbert states he can't possibly get the wiring repaired before Colonel Livingston's reading tonight. And, even if he could, between that and the soaked furniture, I can't possibly get the room in shape for company in just a few short hours."

Lord Browning was leaning against the wall behind Lady Amelia Dallyripple. He made eye contact with Lady Elizabeth and gave a slight nod.

"Amelia, please don't upset yourself. We'd be happy to host Colonel Livingston's book reading tonight." Lady Elizabeth stood and moved to the button beside the fireplace that summoned the butler. "Now, why don't you help yourself to another sandwich and a scone."

Chapter 14

A shadow fell across my laptop screen. I glanced up and found myself gazing into the big blue eyes of Olivia Townsend.

"Am I interrupting?" she said.

I pressed SAVE and lowered the lid of my laptop. "Of course not."

She flashed a smile. It wasn't as blindingly bright as her husband's, but she could definitely get a job as a toothpaste model with any of the major brands. "If you're not too busy, I was hoping maybe we could have a coffee."

Olivia Townsend smiled broadly, but the smile never reached her eyes.

"Sure." I packed away my laptop and grabbed my purse.

We walked toward the room the festival committee had set aside for authors to get tea or coffee and sit for a brief break. The perimeter of the room was lined with folding tables covered by the same black tablecloths that were used in the hallway for the author signings. The university must have invested a small fortune on black tablecloths. On each table, the festival organizers, and some of the authors, had placed business cards, bookmarks, and other swag, along with older books that authors were giving away for free. The inner area of the room held tables with folding chairs. These chairs weren't comfortable enough for long-term habitation, so there was no danger of anyone setting up permanent camp here.

We found a small table near the back of the room and sat.

For several moments, we sat in an awkward silence and sipped our coffee. When the silence became too much, Olivia took a deep breath, plastered on a smile, and said, "I guess you're wondering why I wanted to talk to you."

I went through the motions of denying her claim, but we both knew I wasn't telling the truth, and I quickly stopped. "Well, I have to admit to a certain amount of curiosity, but since I own a bookstore, I find authors sometimes want me to push their books, so . . ."

"I do plan to go to your store this afternoon and sign stock. Both Paul and I will go. Will two o'clock work?"

"I'm sure that will be perfect. Whatever time you can, the books are available. I can also let my grandmother know, and she'll make sure to spread the word. That is, if you would be willing to sign and take pictures with some of your fans."

Olivia nodded her approval, so I pulled out my cell and sent Nana Jo a text. She responded promptly that she would make sure there was a decent number of fans present if she had to go into the alley and pull every homeless person from the street into the store.

I smiled, knowing that she meant every word. "Great. My grandmother is getting the word out."

Olivia took a deep breath. "I also wanted to ask if you knew anything more about what happened to poor Clark. I've heard that you're friends with the local police. They aren't telling us much."

"I wouldn't call Detective Pitt and I friends. In fact, I think if he wasn't a policeman, he'd gladly strangle both me and my grandmother." I chuckled. "He considers us *meddling busybodies.*"

"Oh." She tried to hide the disappointment on her face and glanced around as though she couldn't find the closest exit fast enough.

"We're not friends, but I did talk to him this morning," I said to preempt her making a mad dash for the door.

"Oh?" This time those two letters were full of anticipation and hope as opposed to disappointment.

"I think Detective Pitt was curious if I had any insight that might help him shed a light on the murder."

"So, the police believe it was murder?" she asked. "Everyone is saying Clark Cunningham was murdered, but you know how crowds are. One false bit of information, and a rumor can spread through a crowd like wildfire."

I knew Detective Pitt well enough to know that he wouldn't want me to spread any inside information, but the fact that Clark Cunningham was poisoned wouldn't be something he could keep silent long. "I'm fairly certain that he was poisoned."

"Oh!"

This time there was shock in that one little word. The former English teacher in me marveled at how one word, just two letters, could convey so much simply by the tone and inflection.

"Was it the champagne?" she asked.

I shrugged. "I don't know when or how."

She bit her lower lip and twisted her wedding ring on her finger. She looked into the distance as though she were seeing something in the past or perhaps the future. Wherever Olivia Townsend was mentally, she wasn't here in the present with me. After a few moments, she returned to the here and now. She forced a smile and leaned forward. "I don't suppose you know who the police are targeting?"

"Sorry. Like I said, Detective Pitt doesn't confide in me." Something flashed across her face that I could only call relief. The emotion left as quickly as it appeared, and I was emboldened to ask, "Do you have any ideas?"

She stiffened. "Me? No. I couldn't possibly imagine anyone who would want to see Clark Cunningham dead." She lowered her gaze for a few moments. "I don't suppose the police will believe me after I tossed my drink in his face." She covered her face with her hands. "That was so childish, and I feel awful."

Ah, now we're getting to the heart of the matter.

She lowered her hands and sat up straight. "I was just so furious. Last night was going to be Paul's special night. I just know he was going to win the Best Spy Thriller category. His last book, *Death of a Spy*, was his best book ever. To have him dragged from the room like that . . . well, it wasn't just humiliating, it was criminal. He wouldn't get the honor of going up on stage to receive his award." She closed her eyes and shook her head. "I was furious with Clark. I could have killed—"

I filled in the blanks. "Killed him?"

"I didn't mean it. I would never kill Clark or anyone. It's just a saying."

I liked Olivia Townsend, but I couldn't let this go without comment. "I'm sure you didn't mean it, but you can't joke about things like that in this day and age."

"You're right, and I'll do a better job of watching my mouth." She held up three fingers in the Girl Scouts pledge and forced a grin. "But it doesn't change the fact that I didn't kill Clark Cunningham."

"What did Paul mean by his comments about Judith?" I asked.

Olivia's cheeks flushed. She took a sip of her coffee. "I don't know what you mean."

"He said she'd fooled him and that he wanted to wipe that smile off her face."

"He didn't mean it. He didn't mean anything by it. Paul was just angry because . . ." The flush that made her cheeks red was now covering her entire face.

I reached across the table and squeezed her hand.

Olivia stopped abruptly and burst into tears.

I rummaged through my purse for a handkerchief. Unable to find one, I grabbed the paper napkin from under my coffee cup and slid it across to her.

She took the napkin, wiped her eyes, and blew her nose. When she had herself together, she sniffed. "I'm sorry. I must look a hot mess."

"You're under a lot of strain. Would it help to talk?"

She closed her eyes and took several deep breaths. I couldn't help wondering if she was practicing tactical breathing too. After a few moments, she calmed down enough to add, "I'm sorry. You're right. The last few months have been a strain."

Months? I was just thinking about last night.

"Two years ago, Paul and I went through a . . . low point in our marriage. He moved out, and I, well, things didn't look good and I fell apart. I started taking tranquilizers and, well . . . I got addicted. Then, Judith made a play for him. She practically threw herself at him."

I forced what I hoped was a sympathetic look on my face and nodded. Inside, my brain wasn't buying Paul's innocence. *Sure, she threw herself at him, and he played catcher really well.*

"Paul went through a bit of a writing slump while we were struggling to make our marriage work. Judith came in like a breath of fresh air. She wasn't nagging him to pick up his socks or put the toilet seat down. She sat at his feet and listened to every word he said, no matter how tired she was. She listened."

Uh-huh. I'll bet she listened, but I'll bet he didn't leave his dirty socks on the floor when she came over, either.

"I can't blame Paul. After twenty years of marriage, I'd let myself slip. Yoga pants and a T-shirt became my normal wardrobe. I didn't bother combing my hair or putting on makeup or fancy lingerie to welcome him home anymore. I blame myself for letting the flame burn out."

Okay, Nana Jo always said whatever you do to get your spouse is what you need to do to keep them, but that's a two-way street. I'd bet my favorite pen that Paul West, who wrote books so steamy they made 007 look like a monk, knew where the matches were too.

"So, Judith sailed in and gave him all of the love and attention that I hadn't. She became his muse. With her, he was inspired to write again, and he wrote a great book." She stared into her cup. "It was just like when they were younger and at college together. They had been inseparable back then. Judith, Paul, Nora, and Clark. Nora and Paul were an item back then, but then they broke up and he and I got together. I was in theatre. Back then, I wanted to be an actress. I used to be pretty good. I used to imitate all of the famous actresses, but I switched to English to be with Paul. He's the reason I started writing." She smiled. "We got married not long afterward and we were happy together. That is, until a couple of years ago. Anyway—"

"Wait. Nora Cooper and Clark Cunningham?"

She nodded. "Nora and Clark used to be an item back then. That was before the accident. He—"

"Accident? What accident?"

"I'm sorry. I forget that you're new to the author scene. The crime fiction community is so small, I assume everyone knows everyone else's business." She tilted her head and stared at the ceiling. "First, Nora and Clark were together. Then, he dumped Nora for Judith. Nora and Judith were roommates at the time, so it was horribly awkward."

My head ached as I tried to keep the relationships straight. *Holy moly, Batman!* "Let me get this straight. While Nora and Judith were roommates, Nora was dating Clark."

Olivia nodded. "Nora was head over heels in love with Clark, and we all thought they were well on their way to the altar. Clark was a couple of years older and a successful publicist, and Nora was an aspiring author. It was a match made in heaven."

"But Clark dumped Nora for Judith."

Olivia nodded again. "I guess it sounds a bit like a soap opera, doesn't it? Clark dumped Nora. Then Judith and Clark started dating. Nora didn't take it well."

I rubbed my forehead. *I wonder why.*

"Wow," I said. "Please tell me Nora kicked Judith out."

Olivia shook her head slowly. "Nope. The apartment was Judith's, and I guess Nora didn't have anywhere else to go."

"Geez! I think I would have slept on the street before I stayed there, but . . . to each his own." I took a deep breath. "I'm sorry, please continue."

"Well, Judith and Clark hooked up, and things seemed to be going fairly well. I think Clark was really in love with Judith. She's one of those women who men fall for." She took a deep breath. "Anyway, Clark was involved in a terrible car crash. He nearly lost his life. His back was messed up really badly too. That's when he got started on painkillers. After a while, he was addicted, and his career started down the toilet. That's why Nora was so messed up afterward."

"Wait, I don't understand. Where does Nora Cooper fit into this? I thought she and Clark broke up?"

"Didn't I mention it? Nora caused the accident."

Chapter 15

"How did Nora cause the accident?"

"One evening, Judith and Clark were out driving, and Nora was following them. She used to do crazy stuff like that after the breakup. I guess she must have become a bit unstable."

You think?

"Anyway, according to Judith, Nora deliberately drove her car straight toward them as if she was going to hit them head on. Clark swerved to avoid crashing into her and ran into a tree. Judith walked away with barely a scratch. Clark was lucky he wasn't killed, but he did hurt his back. That's when he started in on the painkillers."

"What happened between him and Judith?" I asked.

"Clark had to go through a lot of physical therapy and had several surgeries. He got addicted to painkillers, and his career spiraled downhill."

She didn't say it, so I did. "And Judith dumped him?"

Olivia shrugged. "She said he changed, and I'm sure he did. I mean, he was on lots of medications and in constant pain, and, well . . . anyway, he and Judith broke up. Nora was on the verge of a breakdown before the accident, but afterward she just lost it. She was never quite the same after the accident. She wasn't physically injured, but she wasn't okay. She spent some time in a mental hospital. While Nora was . . . away, Judith took up with Paul, but then she wrote *The Corpse Danced at Midnight*. After that, her career took off. She dumped Paul." She glanced down into her cup. "He was devastated. Although, I suppose it worked out well for me. I mean, he realized what a fool he'd been, and he came back home. I changed too. I lost weight. Exercised. Got in shape. It was hard, but I did what I had to do to save my marriage."

"And you took him back?" I asked.

"Of course. It wasn't all his fault. I mean, there was more that I could have done to keep the spark going in our marriage. So, that's when I decided to work on myself." She glanced down at her chest. "I'm sure Scarlet told you that I had some work done."

Despite my best effort, I couldn't stop my eyes from moving down to take in her . . . augmentations. "She might have mentioned it."

Olivia laughed. "Don't worry, I know Scarlet MacDunkin well enough to know she had a few choice words to say about me, but I don't care. I love my husband, and my marriage is important. Once I was off the pills, I decided to get some work done. If a few cosmetic enhancements were what it took to keep my husband happy, then I was happy to do it."

I was silent. I didn't know what to say to that. If my late husband Leon or, heaven forbid, Frank dumped me for another woman, and then after he got dumped, he came crawling back, I'm not sure I would want him back. I glanced at Olivia. For an instant, I saw beyond her exterior façade. For a split second, I saw a frightened little girl who was insecure and unsure of herself. Just as I was insecure in my role as an author, Olivia Townsend was also insecure. She'd gone through a terrible ordeal.

"You think I'm foolish, don't you?" Olivia asked.

"No. No, I don't. No one can tell someone what they should do. My Nana Jo always said you can't judge anyone until you've walked in their shoes."

"Nana Jo?"

"My grandmother."

"She sounds like a wise woman."

"She is, and I'm very lucky to have her, but back to the story. What happened between Nora and Judith?"

"Nora claimed that *The Corpse Danced at Midnight* was her book. She said Judith stole her manuscript. Well, you can imagine how that came across. Judith stole her man, then she stole her manuscript."

"Do you believe her?"

She thought about the question. "Not really. I mean, Nora was never that great of a writer. Her books were . . . entertaining, but nothing like *The Corpse Danced at Midnight*. In all honesty, I think it's just sour grapes."

"It seems there are quite a few people here who have a reason to dislike Judith Hunter," I said. "I mean, Nora Cooper claims she stole her boyfriend and her manuscript. Clark Cunningham was dumped by Judith during his most vulnerable time. And Paul . . ." I let the sentence hang in the air.

"But Paul didn't feel bitter toward Judith. He came home. We saved our marriage, and we've never been happier. His career is doing well, and I feel confident he's going to win the Best Spy Thriller award. He was just spouting off last night because he had a bit too much to drink. Trust me. Paul wasn't pining after Judith Hunter, and he certainly didn't try to kill her." She stood up. "And you can tell that police detective that too." She grabbed her purse and marched out of the room.

Wow. Methinks the lady doth protest too much.

I sat alone for several minutes after she left and tried to process everything she'd said. If Clark Cunningham had dated both Nora and Judith, then both women may have wanted to kill him. At least Nora would. Nora Cooper had a motive for wanting both Clark Cunningham and Judith Hunter dead. Did Nora Cooper deliberately kill Clark Cunningham? Or, did she attempt to kill Judith Hunter and inadvertently killed Clark Cunningham? Either way, Nora Cooper had a strong motive. If her target was Judith Hunter, would she try again?

Chapter 16

My head was spinning. I glanced at my watch. I had an hour before my next panel. I needed to think, so I pulled out my laptop and started to write.

~⁓~

Wickfield Lodge, Drawing Room

Thompkins, Mrs. McDuffie, and the entire Marsh family staff did a fantastic job getting Wickfield Lodge ready at short notice for a book reading. Lady Elizabeth walked through the drawing room and nodded at the arrangements. The sofa and chairs were arranged around the fireplace with a place of prominence left for the speaker.

Mrs. Anderson, normally temperamental, especially when called upon to adjust her routine to accommodate last-minute guests, was surprisingly helpful. Lady Elizabeth couldn't help but wonder if

Charlotte Granger's unexpected termination had anything at all to do with it. Regardless, she wasn't one to look a gift horse in the mouth.

Lord William Marsh was still a bit put out by the change to his routine. However, Lady Elizabeth knew he would play host when the time came.

The drawing room door opened, and Lord William entered. "Elizabeth, I can't get this blasted collar right."

Lady Elizabeth walked over and adjusted her husband's tie and fixed his collar. When she finished, she kissed his nose. "There. Now you look fit to visit the king."

Lord William smiled.

The door opened, and Lord James Browning entered, followed by his best friend and brother-in-law, Lord Victor Carlston.

"Victor, I'm so glad you and Penelope were able to make it at such short notice," Lady Elizabeth said and kissed her nephew's cheek.

"Our pleasure."

Lady Elizabeth glanced around. "Where's Penelope?"

"Right here." Lady Penelope hurried into the room. She greeted her aunt and uncle and then turned to her brother-in-law. "How's Daphne? I wish she could have made the trip."

Lord James Browning reassured Penelope that all was well and that Daphne sent her love.

Lady Elizabeth gazed at her family and smiled. Daphne and Penelope were complete opposites in looks. Lady Penelope was tall and slender, with dark hair and eyes. Between the two sisters, she bore the strongest resemblance to their late mother, Lady

Henrietta Pringle. Daphne was petite, with blond hair and blue eyes, like their father, Lord Peregrine Marsh. Despite their differences, the sisters were both beautiful, and Lady Elizabeth couldn't help but be thankful that both had made great matches.

Lord Victor Carlston was the Earl of Lochloren. He was thirty, tall, dark, and handsome. The Marshes had known Victor since his youth when he mistakenly believed himself in love with Daphne. Fortunately, Penelope had helped him realize where his true heart belonged, and now the two lived happily with their son and heir, Lord William Peregrine Carlston. Soon, the young lord would have a cousin. Lady Elizabeth closed her eyes and sent up a prayer of thanks for her family.

Victor leaned against the fireplace and smoked. "Now, what's with this book reading?"

"Don't ask me," Lord William said, puffing on his pipe. "I just live here."

Before Lady Elizabeth could explain, Thompkins entered and announced Lady Dallyripple and Colonel Livingston's arrival.

Lady Elizabeth didn't know what to expect. Most men, including her husband and both of her nephews, had been in the military. However, Colonel Livingston was a tall man with a red face and prominent mustache. His hair was thin and stood at attention whenever he made a sudden move that caught the wind.

He entered the room as though he were marching into battle. He snapped to attention and bowed to Lady Elizabeth.

Lady Elizabeth offered her hand.

Colonel Basil Livingston raised her hand to his lips.

Lady Dallyripple snickered. "Isn't he gallant? Men never kiss a lady's hand anymore."

"For good reason," Lady Penelope whispered just loud enough for everyone to hear.

Lady Dallyripple took the colonel's arm and escorted him around the room, introducing him to each person.

Thompkins entered. Coughed. And announced, "Reverend and Mrs. Baker."

The vicar and his wife entered. Mrs. Baker was a lovely woman, although she was slightly deaf in her right ear and tended to speak rather loudly.

Thompkins returned and announced, "Sebastian Lloyd, Oliver Birdwhistle, and Sir Greyson Bythesea."

The three men entered. The last, a rotund man with a red face, stopped. "It's Bither-see."

Thompkins bowed. "I beg your pardon."

Lady Dallyripple laughed. "Oh, Elizabeth. You know Oliver Birdwhistle and Sir Greyson. They're both members of the House of Commons. Conservatives, of course." She grinned. "I was fortunate to get so many distinguished men to agree to judge our little village baking contest, but I don't think you've met Colonel Livingston's secretary, Sebastian Lloyd. When I heard you had invited the vicar and his wife, I invited Sebastian to make the table even. It's bad luck to have an odd number."

Lady Elizabeth wondered if there was more behind Lady Dallyripple's water catastrophe. Did she really need to move the dinner and book reading because of water damage? Or, was she attempting to

force Mrs. Anderson to appear in a less than flattering light to the judges by forcing this last-minute dinner party, thus saving her French chef as a surprise
for tomorrow's event? Lady Elizabeth wouldn't put it
past Lady Dallyripple to plan something like that. She
was desperate to win the contest.

Lady Elizabeth nodded. "Of course, Amelia. We're
pleased to have all of you here. I just need to make
sure that another setting is placed at the table. Please
excuse me."

Colonel Livingston turned to Lord William. "What's
an old soldier need to do to get a drink around here?"

Lady Elizabeth slipped out and hurried downstairs
to the kitchen, which was in a frenzy. The maids scurried about, while the footmen, Jim and Frank, tugged
at their collars in their fancy formal attire.

Mrs. Anderson hollered, "How did we go from a
simple family supper to a blooming seven-course
meal in just a few hours?"

"Mrs. Anderson!" Thompkins yelled.

The cook noticed Lady Elizabeth for the first time.
"I'm sorry, your ladyship."

Lady Elizabeth waved her hand. "No need to apologize. It's I who should be apologizing to you."

The cook lowered her head. "Your ladyship don't
owe me no apology. I'm just letting off a bit of steam.
I'll make sure the meal is a credit to the Marsh family.
Don't you worry none about that."

"I was thinking maybe we could make things easier and just do five courses instead of seven," Lady
Elizabeth said.

Mrs. Anderson stood up straight and narrowed
her eyes. "Not on my watch. We won't be serving less
than seven courses at a dinner party in Wickfield

Lodge. I begs your ladyship's pardon, but don't you worry none about the food."

The cook turned and walked to the back of the kitchen to the large AGA stove, mumbling that no one would be getting less than seven courses and that she'd make sure everyone had plenty of food, even if she had to go out and shoot the pheasants herself.

"Well, if you're sure," Lady Elizabeth said. She turned and gave a knowing look to Mrs. McDuffie before leaving.

Chapter 17

"Sam!"

I blinked as I forced my mind back from 1939 England to the present. I glanced up and into the eyes of Dorothy Clark. "I'm sorry. I was lost in my book." I pressed SAVE and closed my laptop.

"I figured you were miles away. I just wanted to let you know that Jacob arranged everything. In fact, he said if I wrote the article, he'd print it," Dorothy said with a tinge of uncertainty in her voice.

"That's great. Isn't it?"

"I suppose, but it's been years since I wrote anything. Decades. Journalism has changed since I went to school."

"Good journalism is the same today as it's always been. Who, what, where, when, why, and how are still the six most important questions. At least, that's what I was taught in college when I worked on the school paper."

"That's exactly what Jacob said too. He's always looking for good articles and even offered to let me freelance for him, if I can bring him something good." Dorothy sat down in the seat Olivia Townsend had vacated. "He's a journalism purist, and he said it's amazing how many people struggle to write coherent sentences. Not only do they not know proper sentence structure, but they don't worry about fact-checking anymore."

"Do you want to freelance?" I asked.

"I don't know. I don't need the money, but it might be fun to stay busy." Dorothy shrugged. "Well, I'm here, and I've got my press credentials." She held up a badge hanging from a lanyard around her neck. "Where's my principal?"

"Principal?"

"You know, principal . . . the person I'm protecting."

"Oh, Judith. Judith Hunter."

"They call them a principal on that British cop show with that drop-dead gorgeous actor, Idris Elba. *Grrr.*"

I chuckled and pulled the festival program out of my bag. I flipped it open and glanced at the schedule. "According to this, Judith Hunter should be just preparing for a Q and A in the auditorium." I glanced at the time. "If we hurry, we should be able to catch her before she goes on stage."

We arrived at the backstage door to the auditorium in time to hear another argument featuring Judith Hunter, Scarlet MacDunkin, and Nora Cooper. Instead of Clark Cunningham, Detective Pitt was the sole male participant. Dorothy and I stopped outside of the room and listened.

"You have got to be kidding!" Judith Hunter said. "No way. Absolutely no way."

"My job is to serve and protect," Detective Pitt said. "The best way I can do my job is if we shut down this festival until we find out who murdered Clark Cunningham. Now, I just need a little cooperation, and we can—"

"Detective Pitt, I have no intention of leaving this book festival. My fans have had to travel to this little backwater town in the middle of nowhere that doesn't even have an airport. I have no intention of disappointing them by running home with my tail tucked between my legs because you *think* someone may have it out for me. I'm tougher than that." Judith Hunter's voice rang out, and I had to stop myself from applauding.

"It's not all about you, Judith," Nora said. "Clark is dead."

"Thanks, Captain Obvious. I must have forgotten that when I was watching my friend and former lover writhing on the ground."

There was a yelp and then what sounded like a scuffle. I glanced at Dorothy, who shoved me aside and wrenched the door open.

Dorothy rushed into the room. Detective Pitt was between the two women, and Nora Cooper had a handful of Judith Hunter's hair, while Judith had one hand on her hair to prevent it from being ripped from her scalp and was swinging punches at Nora with the other.

Scarlet MacDunkin was snapping pictures with her phone, an evil grin on her face.

Dorothy assessed the situation. She came up behind Nora and wrapped an arm around her neck. Then, with a sudden twist of Nora's wrist, Dorothy forced Nora to release Judith's hair.

Nora screamed in pain and dropped to her knees, but Dorothy did not release her arm until she glanced over her shoulder and saw that Detective Pitt had control of Judith.

"If you behave I'll let you go," Dorothy said. "Now, are you going to play nice?"

Nora Cooper whimpered.

"I'll take that as a yes." Dorothy released Nora's arm, but her stance indicated that if Nora made a move, she'd soon find herself tied up like a calf at a rodeo.

"She killed Clark. I know she did." Nora glared at Dorothy, but then leaned her head down on the ground and howled. "It should have been you, not Clark."

"Sam, help me get her up." Dorothy was tough, but she wasn't mean.

Between the two of us, we lifted Nora up and got her seated in a chair. Dorothy kept an eye on Judith in case she planned a counterattack. However, Judith merely glowered at Nora as she massaged her scalp and paced at the opposite end of the room.

Still wearing a wicked smirk, Scarlet took a few last photos. She walked to a corner and began swiping her cell phone. However, she made the tactical mistake of turning her back on Judith Hunter.

Judith made a mad dash toward Scarlet and snatched the phone from her hand.

"Hey, gimme that!" Scarlet yelled.

"Detective, stop her," Judith said.

For a split second, Detective Pitt looked confused. However, when Scarlet lunged at Judith in an attempt to recover her phone, his reflexes finally kicked in. He grabbed Scarlet around the waist and pulled her away.

In a previous life, Scarlet must have spent time on a boat, because she spewed out a series of expletives that might have made a sailor blush.

"If you don't let go of me right now, I'm going to—"

The door burst open, and we never got to hear what Scarlet intended to do to Detective Pitt. Standing in the doorway were Mrs. Graves and two uniformed security guards.

Mrs. Graves looked around the room. "What on earth is going on in here?"

Guarded by Dorothy, Nora Cooper sat sobbing in a chair. Scarlet MacDunkin was being held in a bear hug by Detective Pitt while she kicked, screamed, and spewed obscenities, and Judith Hunter was frantically deleting pictures from Scarlet's phone.

"Detective Pitt, would you please unhand that woman,"

Mrs. Graves said. She spoke softly, but there was steel in her words that brooked no opposition.

Detective Pitt released Scarlet but kept one eye on her and one hand near the holster on the right side of his body.

"There," Judith said. "All done." She tossed Scarlet's cell phone back.

"You deleted my pictures, you dirty rotten bi—"

"Ladies!" Mrs. Graves said. "This is a university of higher education, not a low-class bordello. You will all behave in a respectful manner or you will be forcibly removed." She glanced at each woman. "All of you."

Mrs. Graves was a woman of authority who was accustomed to obedience. She got it. Each woman lowered their gaze, and the tension decreased three hundred percent. She gave a slight nod to the security guards and they left.

Satisfied, Mrs. Graves turned to Detective Pitt. "Now, can someone tell me exactly what is going on in here?"

Detective Pitt turned to me.

"Mrs. Graves, I honestly don't know. We just arrived and saw . . ." I looked down at Nora Cooper, who had shriveled up and was rocking in her chair.

Scarlet MacDunkin stepped forward. "I'll tell you what's going on. Detective Manhandler here was trying to convince Her Majesty to cancel her appearance at the book festival to prevent another murder."

Detective Pitt found his voice. "I'm just doing my duty. I have reason to believe that Miss Hunter may be in danger. Poison was found in the glass of champagne that she gave to Clark Cunningham. That was her glass. Someone deliberately attempted to kill Judith Hunter. That person might just try again."

Mrs. Graves turned to Judith. "Well?"

"I'm not going anywhere."

"Your stubbornness is going to lead to another innocent

person losing their life," Nora sneered, and then she retreated back into her own world.

Judith paced from one end of the room to the other. "Terrorists. That's how they work. Don't you see? There's no way terrorists can win. They're outnumbered. Their goal is to frighten people. They want to keep you afraid to go on airplanes or attend public events. There's no way they could hurt everyone. There aren't enough of them. They win by getting us to alter our lives. We stop going on vacations. Stop attending concerts, marathons . . ." She stopped pacing and stared at Detective Pitt. "We stop going to book festivals. We retreat into our own cocoons and stop living. That's what they want. That's how they win. Well, it won't work. I refuse to be intimidated by some coward."

There was a long pause of silence while we digested Judith's comments. The silence was broken when Scarlet Mac-Dunkin clapped.

"Bravo," Scarlet said.

"Oh, shut up," Judith said.

Mrs. Graves turned back to Detective Pitt.

"Well, after Miss Hunter made a comment," Detective Pitt said, "Miss Cooper—"

Scarlet stepped forward. "After Judith refused, she made an inconsiderate comment about Clark's death, which Nora took exception to. Nora went for Judith. Detective Pitt got in the middle, and then Sam and the Amazon Queen of Martial Arts busted in and broke it up. I tried to document the altercation, and Judith stole my phone and deleted the evidence."

"You liar!" Judith yelled.

"I call 'em as I see 'em."

Judith looked as though she was about to protest, but Mrs. Graves held up a hand to halt the rebuttal. "I think I have the picture." She turned to Dorothy. "And who are you?"

"Dorothy Clark. I'm a freelance reporter here to do an article on Miss Hunter." Dorothy held up her badge and press pass.

"Miss MacDunkin, I don't believe you're in this next panel," Mrs. Graves said. At least those were the words that came out of her mouth. However, her facial expression said, *You are simply here to cause trouble, and you need to move on.*

Scarlet read the expression and knew exactly what it meant. She took her cell phone and purse and exited the room stage right.

"Detective Pitt, I understand your desire to ensure that Miss Hunter is safe," Mrs. Graves said. "However, I believe she has made her position clear." She turned to Judith, who nodded her agreement. "I have also discussed your request to cancel the remainder of the book festival with the committee. While we appreciate your concerns, we have unanimously agreed that the festival will continue."

Detective Pitt started to speak but was halted by Mrs. Graves. "We have, however, agreed to postpone the awards banquet one more day to allow you and your team time to catch the killer."

"One day? How am I supposed to catch a killer in one day?"

"That, Detective Pitt, is not my problem." Mrs. Graves gave him a frosty stare that made me shiver. Then she turned her attention to Nora Cooper, who sat with her arms wrapped around her torso, rocking and humming. "I think Miss Cooper has suffered quite enough over the last couple of days and would benefit from medical attention and rest." She glanced around the room. She must have realized that pickings were slim when it came to suitable helpers. Finally, her gaze landed on me. "Mrs. Washington. If it's not too much of an inconvenience, would you help Miss Cooper to the infirmary. Someone as . . . empathetic as she is must be overcome by all of the negative energy."

Nora Cooper looked up at Mrs. Graves like a puppy.

Detective Pitt snorted.

"I'll be more than happy to help," I said. I wrapped my arms around Nora's waist and helped her stand. Together, we slowly headed to the door.

Mrs. Graves glanced at Dorothy. "I will leave you to your interview." She turned on her heel and walked out.

Chapter 18

The campus infirmary wasn't far from the administration building, which was a good thing because I wasn't sure if Nora Cooper would have made it more than a block. We walked slowly, and I supported most of her weight. I was grateful that when we got to the lobby, I found a wheelchair and eased Nora down into it.

I approached the front desk of the infirmary. "Hi. Mrs. Graves asked—"

"We've been expecting you." The woman pushed a buzzer and two men came from the back.

"Is this Miss Cooper?" one of the men asked.

"Yes. I was—"

They pushed the wheelchair with Nora Cooper through a set of double doors, leaving me staring at the closed doors. I turned back to the woman behind the desk. "Do I need to do anything?"

She looked at me as though I were speaking a foreign language.

"You know, fill out forms? Paperwork? Not that I know the answers to any of the questions to complete them, but . . .

whenever I've gone to a hospital or even my dentist's office, they always ask five million questions."

"Mrs. Graves will take care of the paperwork." She typed on her computer.

"Should I stay? I'd hate to just leave her here alone."

"Only immediate family members allowed." She must have had some compassion because she hesitated and then added, "Why don't you give us a call later after the doctor has had a chance to look her over. There's nothing you can do for her right now."

She was right. Nora Cooper's nerves were shot, and my standing there wasn't going to help her in the least. It's not like I was family or even a close friend. I'd only met the woman yesterday.

I walked back over to the administration building. I had several hours until my next panel, so I had time to catch the tail end of Judith Hunter's interview before I needed to be anywhere.

The auditorium was packed. There were kids sitting on the floor in the aisles and standing up near the back, violating all fire-safety rules. I elbowed my way to a corner near the wall where I could see the stage. My position gave me a side view of Judith and a sliver of the backstage crew. Dorothy Clark towered over everyone else, making her easy to spot.

I risked the ire of my fellow standing-room-only compatriots and jostled my way back the way I came and out of the auditorium. I hurried backstage and found Dorothy. I moved beside her.

"What did I miss?" I whispered.

"Not much. I'm going to interview her after she finishes this presentation and signs more books."

Dorothy kept her eyes focused on Judith. She was taking her role of bodyguard seriously.

After the interview, Dorothy reinforced her role by snapping pictures of the audience during their standing ovation.

I spotted Detective Pitt as we were heading to the hallway. When we made eye contact, he developed a tic. Either the detective wanted to talk to me privately or he was having a stroke.

I straggled back and then slipped into the backstage room I'd seen the detective enter moments earlier. It took a great deal of self-control not to glance around to make sure no one saw me, but I forced myself.

I pushed open the door and found Detective Pitt waiting for me.

"One day," he said. "Can you believe it? That old biddy's only giving me one day to figure out who tried to kill Judith Hunter? I'm not a magician. I can't just wave my magic wand and conjure up a killer. That's not how police work is."

"Do you have any clues?" I asked.

"No. Do you?"

I shared the conversation I had earlier with Olivia Townsend.

"Wait, so Nora Cooper and Clark Cunningham were an item until Judith Hunter stole him from her? Then Judith dumps him, steals her manuscript, and makes a fortune with it?"

We were both so intent on our conversation, neither of us noticed when Judith Hunter entered the room.

"I did *NOT* steal Nora's manuscript."

Judith waltzed into the room. She went to a table and picked up a pair of reading glasses. She held them up. "I came back for my glasses, but we might as well get something straight. I repeat. I did not steal Nora Cooper's manuscript." She folded her arms across her chest. "I bought it."

Chapter 19

The shock of Judith's revelation must have damaged my hearing. I shook my head like one of my poodles and squinted as if that would help me hear better. "Wait. What? How?"

Dorothy pushed the door open and was about to enter when Judith stopped her. "Would you mind waiting outside? We're having a private conversation."

"Of course, I'll be right outside," Dorothy said, and backed out of the room, closing the door behind her.

We turned our attention back to Judith.

"Look, this is confidential, and if either of you blabs one word of it, I'll sue you for every dime you ever made." Judith glared from me to Detective Pitt and then back to me again.

I crossed my heart, zipped my lips, and tossed the invisible key over my shoulder.

Judith took a deep breath. "Nora Cooper and I used to be friends. Good friends. We were roommates." She glared at me. "I guess you know that already if you found out about me and Clark."

I nodded.

"She used to be really talented. That manuscript was good.

She'd started it in college and then let it sit. She never finished it. It was good. Not great, but good. And I wanted it. I knew that with a little work, it could be great." Judith paced. "I knew Clark had the hots for me. He was dating Nora, but he wasn't in love with her. Part of me wanted to show her. I wanted to prove that he didn't really care about her. So . . . I made a play for him."

I've never been good at hiding my feelings, and my distaste must have shown on my face.

"Oh, don't give me that holier-than-thou look. I did Nora a favor. If he hadn't dumped her for me, it would have been someone else." She paced a few more times to recover her composure. "She was devastated. I thought . . . I thought she would be angry. Upset. But I had no idea she would go cuckoo for Cocoa Puffs. Something inside snapped, and she was all Glenn-Close-mess-with-me-and-I'll-boil-your-rabbit bonkers."

Detective Pitt frowned. "What?"

Judith rolled her eyes.

"*Fatal Attraction.* It's a movie that came out in the late nineteen eighties," I said. It had been a while since I'd seen the film, but that scene was certainly memorable.

"What's a boiled bunny got to do with Nora Cooper?" Detective Pitt scratched his head. "I don't get it."

"Google it," I suggested, and then returned my attention to Judith Hunter. "Then what happened?"

"Then, there was the accident. It was all her fault. She had been following us and deliberately drove her car toward us. Clark had to swerve to avoid hitting her. The impact threw me clear, but Clark . . . well, he wasn't so lucky. If I thought Nora was nuts before, I was wrong. Before she was teetering on the edge, but that accident sent her all the way into the deep end." She paused.

"What happened?" I asked.

"She needed help, serious mental health help. I felt kind of responsible. Nora didn't have a pot to pee in. The state mental health hospital was medieval. So, I paid to have her placed in a private facility. My dad was one of the doctors there, so I was able to get her in at a discounted rate. She got great care, and after a few years, she was finally well enough to be released."

"I don't understand. When did she sell you her book?"

Judith flushed. "She knew she couldn't afford that facility and all of the care she was getting. It was really nice."

This sounded like a setup, so I merely listened.

"One day, when she was doing a lot better, I went to see her. I explained how expensive the facility was, and I told her that if she signed over all rights to *The Corpse Danced at Midnight*, that I'd call it even."

I wondered if a contract signed by someone in a mental institution would be considered legal. I made a mental note to check with Jenna. "So, she signed the papers in the mental hospital?"

Judith nodded. "She signed. I had a lawyer draw up the papers so everything would be legal. Nora agreed that she wouldn't talk about it. She didn't care about the book. It wasn't published, and there were no guarantees that anyone would ever publish it. Even if it got published, there was still no guarantee that it would sell many copies, so it was a good deal."

"But she did talk," I said.

"Yeah. Everything was fine until the book became this mega hit. That's when she started spouting off about how I stole her book. She broke our contract. My lawyers said I could sue her. But . . ."

"But, if you did, you'd have to admit that you hadn't actually written the book."

Judith scowled. "I own that book. I bought it fair and

square. And I had to make changes to it. I added my own spin. I changed the names and moved it from Minnesota to Michigan. I worked hard on that manuscript, and it's mine."

"Where does Clark Cunningham come into all of this?" Detective Pitt said, surprising me by cutting straight to the heart of the matter.

"After the accident, Clark got addicted to painkillers. He barely remembered his name. He certainly didn't remember Nora's book. But then he got clean. Between his memory returning and Nora's constant interference, I guess he must have remembered her manuscript." She shrugged. "I don't know, but the bottom line is that I did not put cyanide in Clark Cunningham's drink. Nor did I steal Nora Cooper's book, and if anyone says I did, then you'd better be ready for a very long and expensive legal battle." Judith gave each of us an evil scowl. "Now, I have books to sign." She turned and marched out of the room.

Detective Pitt and I stood in silence for a few moments while the air pressure returned to normal. Judith Hunter was a force to be reckoned with. I couldn't get the thought out of my mind that if Nora Cooper went to battle with her, she'd better be prepared to fight to the death.

Chapter 20

"Well?" Detective Pitt turned to me. "Nora Cooper certainly had a good reason to want Judith Hunter and Clark Cunningham dead, but did she do it?"

I shrugged.

"You need to get busy. You heard what that battle axe said, I've only got one day to catch the killer." He pointed at me. "That means *you* only have one day."

"And what are you going to be doing while I'm figuring out who tried to kill Judith Hunter?"

"I'm going to get some additional security." He reached the door and stopped. "Wait. What's that jolly-old-giant woman really doing here? She's no journalist."

I explained that I'd asked Dorothy to stick close to Judith and serve as a bodyguard.

Detective Pitt snorted. "Bodyguard? That old crone?"

"Dorothy Clark is no crone. She's an intelligent, talented, independent woman who happens to be an expert in two different forms of martial arts."

He snorted again.

"Plus, she doesn't scream security, like a uniformed officer would, and she's already started to gain Judith's trust. That's something you'll never do with your bull-in-the-china-shop approach." I marched past Detective Pitt, flung the door open, and walked out.

I was halfway down the hall before my steam petered out. I paused to note the long line of people waiting for Judith to sign their books. Standing next to her was Dorothy Clark. She had her cell phone out and was snapping pictures. She was a born actress. I had no doubt she'd make sure that Judith Hunter was safe.

I kept walking to the end of the hall and turned the corner to my nook.

"Samantha!"

I lifted my head in time to avoid a collision with Scarlet MacDunkin.

"I'm so sorry," I said.

"You were deep in thought, a million miles away."

"True, but I'm so used to nobody being back here in the burbs that I wasn't watching where I was going."

"You're definitely on the outskirts of the action back here."

"Well, it's certainly peaceful." I smiled. "Now, were you looking for me, the men's room, or the fire escape?"

"You. How about lunch? You're local. I'd love to see your bookstore and hopefully grab some food that doesn't come from a college commissary."

I glanced at the time. I had four hours until I was expected at a Q and A about traditional vs. indie publishing. "Sure. Let's swing by my bookstore, and then we can walk down to Frank's restaurant."

We trudged out to the back nine where I'd parked, and I drove the short distance to downtown North Harbor. I suspected that Scarlet didn't care one Fig Newton about North

Harbor's history, but I spouted it off like a tour guide en route.

I pulled into the garage and walked through the back of the building. It wasn't until we entered the actual bookstore that I felt Scarlet showed genuine interest and . . . respect.

"What an adorable bookstore," she said. "I was expecting one of those dark, dusty, moldy-smelling stores crammed full of used books." Scarlet glanced around. "But this has really got a lot of charm. It's light, bright, and cozy."

"Thanks."

The store wasn't packed, but there were quite a few people. My twin nephews, Christopher and Zaq, were home visiting from Chicago for the weekend and were both helping at the counter.

Christopher and Zaq were identical twins. Both were over six feet tall and slender. They had similar features, but at twenty-one, their personalities made them easily identifiable. Christopher was the conservative marketing expert who helped with marketing both me and my store. Zaq was edgier and my technology expert who kept my website, point-of-sale system, and laptop running smoothly. Neither were mystery readers, but whenever they were free, they were willing to help out their favorite, albeit only, aunt.

Nana Jo was helping a customer in the young adult mystery section. Nana Jo looked up and saw us. "Why look, it's bestselling author Scarlet MacDunkin."

Everyone turned and glanced in our direction.

Scarlet froze, but then she smiled and waved.

Christopher pulled a sign from beneath the counter that had Scarlet's face and a picture of her latest book, which I felt sure he had printed. He placed it on the table.

Nana Jo motioned for us to move forward to the table, where she placed a stack of Scarlet's books.

Scarlet sat behind the table, picked up a pen, and prepared to sign.

Christopher directed the crowd to bring their books to the counter to be checked out and then take them over to the table for signatures.

After each purchase, I noticed that Christopher took a Post-it note and jotted down each person's name. He then stuck the Post-it onto the front of the book to help Scarlet know the correct way to address each book.

Zaq snapped a picture of each person with Scarlet and the book. He then had each person write their email address on a clipboard and sent the picture to them via email. The process went like a well-oiled machine.

Nana Jo and I stood by and watched.

"I didn't realize we had so many copies of Scarlet's books," I whispered.

"We didn't. I had your distributor bring a carton of books for each of your prime suspects."

"How? It usually takes days to get books."

"I would tell you, but then I'd have to kill you." Nana Jo smiled.

I kissed my grandmother's cheek.

It didn't take long for Scarlet to get through the crowd. When she was done, I had her sign all of the stock.

"We're going to lunch at Frank's," I said. "Shall I bring you all back something?"

The twins were always hungry. Zaq grinned. "I created an app for Uncle Frank so that he can get online orders. I already sent ours. They'll be ready when you leave."

Hearing my nephews refer to Frank as "uncle" made me tear up. I kissed both him and Christopher and thanked them for their help. Then, Scarlet and I headed down the street.

★   ★   ★

When we got to the restaurant, Frank was working behind the bar. He grinned when he saw me.

There was a crowd, as usual, but when the hostess saw me, she waved me to the front. "I have your table ready."

We followed her to a table near the back. "I'm sorry we didn't have something up front, but we just got your nephew's message that you were coming with a friend."

I reassured her that this was perfect.

We settled in, and Scarlet glanced around the crowded restaurant. "This is nice. I have to admit I was a little nervous. The things I've read about North Harbor haven't been flattering."

I explained more about the history of North Harbor, and that while it had experienced a decline, the city was turning around.

Frank brought a pitcher of lemon water and two glasses to the table. He kissed me and then smiled at Scarlet. "Welcome." Before he finished talking, a waitress arrived with two cups of corn chowder and two BLTs. One without the T.

"Wow," Scarlet said. "That looks delicious. Do you have ESP? How did you know?"

Frank chuckled. "When I got Zaq's order, I started cooking, but you don't have to eat this. I'll be happy to make you anything you'd like." He reached for Scarlet's plate.

Scarlet gave his hand a playful smack. "Touch this plate and you'll be taking away a nub."

Frank held up both hands in surrender. "Would you like something more than water to drink?"

We both declined.

"Enjoy." He winked at me and then returned to the bar.

"That's service." Scarlet tasted the soup and purred. "Yum, delicious."

"I love all of Frank's food, but this is my absolute favorite." I took a spoonful of the soup, closed my eyes, and savored the creamy goodness.

We ate in silence for several moments. Eventually, Scarlet sat back. "That was amazing."

"Frank will be thrilled. He loves to cook," I said with pride.

"Tall, dark, handsome, and he cooks? You are one lucky girl."

We chatted briefly about food and books and eventually Scarlet got to the heart of why she wanted to talk to me.

"I was wondering if you'd made any progress in figuring out who tried to kill Judith Hunter," she said.

"Detective Pitt is—"

"A buffoon. He couldn't solve a mystery if the killer was caught red-handed on camera in front of ten thousand witnesses."

Nana Jo, the girls, and I criticized and mocked Detective Pitt mercilessly. However, we were locals. He represented North Harbor, and I wasn't about to stand idly by while an outsider criticized him. Detective Pitt may have been a bit slow on the uptake, but he had dedicated his life to serving and protecting. Plus, he did save my life and deserved some loyalty, if not respect. "Detective Pitt isn't as clueless as he pretends to be."

"Pretends?"

"Sure. He's like a twenty-first-century edition of Columbo. It's all an act."

"The nineteen-seventies polyester with the pathetic comb-over is all an act?"

"He wants people to think he's clueless. It makes people lower their guard, and then he just swoops in, and that's how he gets his murderer. Every time." Under the table, I crossed my fingers.

"That man deserves an Academy Award." Scarlet still

looked as though she didn't believe me, but she shook it off. "So, who does he think did it?"

"He doesn't confide in me." Something in her attitude made me ask, "Are you afraid he thinks you may have done it?"

I expected the acid-tongued author to attack, but she must have been really worried because she looked down into her empty soup bowl for several moments. "He'd have to be a complete idiot if he hadn't figured out that Judith and I . . ."

"Don't get along?"

"I was going to say hate each other's guts."

"Why?"

She paused so long I thought she wasn't going to answer. Eventually, she said, "She ruined my career."

"How? I mean, you're a successfully published author. You have—"

"Nothing. I'm with a small publisher that doesn't pay advances, does nothing to promote my books, and my royalties are barely enough to pay for a tank of gas."

"But . . . I'm sorry. I know publishing doesn't pay a lot, but you're here at this book festival, and your books have been on some bestseller lists." I racked my brain to remember which lists, but her website said bestselling author.

"You've been reading my website."

"Guilty, but what does Judith have to do with any of that?"

"Judith and I used to be friends—good friends. We were both ambitious. I got my book deal first. Judith pretended she was happy for me. I should have known better, but back then, I was young and dumb enough to believe her act." She took a few deep breaths and then continued. "It was after she broke up with Clark. He'd told her about this guy he knew who had a scheme to help authors get on all of the biggest bestseller lists."

"How is that possible? I mean, the bestseller list means you have to sell a lot of books."

She gave me that *You poor, pitiful thing* look. "Honey, for the right amount of money, you can buy just about anything."

My mouth dropped open, and I quickly shut it. I leaned forward. "Do you mean, bribery?"

"No, no. It's not that simple."

"Oh." I felt grateful that my illusions weren't completely dashed, but I was surprisingly hesitant to learn the dirty truth. Still, I felt compelled to keep going. "Then, how?"

"You own a bookstore. You report sales, right?"

I nodded.

"If you signed up as a client, he arranged to buy large quantities of books from stores around the country that all reported the sales. He claimed he was a buyer for a conference, and the books were shipped to different warehouses where major conferences were being held. I paid for the books, and he got a large commission."

"In order to make most lists, don't you need to buy thousands of books?"

She nodded.

"But, if you weren't getting an advance, then how . . . ?"

"How could I afford it? I couldn't. I took out loans, maxed out all of my credit cards, and pawned everything I could. I was in debt up to my eyeballs."

"Why?"

"To make the list. I figured if I could make the list, then publishers would be falling over themselves to sign me." She snorted.

"So, it didn't work?"

"Oh, it worked. It worked for about two days. I hit the bestseller list. Then, reviewers started questioning how a complete unknown had a book that made it atop one of the most prestigious lists in the country, but no one in the industry had heard of me or my book. That's when they started an investigation and found out what he was doing. It was a huge mess, and they stripped my bestseller title."

"But what does Judith have to do with any of that?"

"She was the one who tipped off the reviewers. She ratted me out."

Chapter 21

"If you two were friends . . . why would she do that?"

"Because she's evil. Judith Hunter is a cruel, evil witch. She is incapable of any decent emotions like friendship, loyalty, or love."

Clearly, Scarlet MacDunkin was bitter, but that didn't mean she was wrong. "There had to be some other reason."

"You'd need to ask her that one."

"Are you sure it was Judith?"

"Absolutely. I made it my business to find out who turned me in. Before I filed for bankruptcy, I sold my grandmother's wedding ring to pay for a private investigator to track down the truth. He brought me photos of the documents with her name on them. It was her alright. My best friend, Judith Hunter, stabbed me in the back. So, if your Detective Pitt wants to know who had a reason to want Judith Hunter dead, he won't have to look far." Scarlet's eyes narrowed, and she looked ready to manhandle a tiger.

My throat was dry. My hand shook as I reached for my glass of lemon water.

Frank must have seen my fear because he came over to the table. "Is everything okay?"

Scarlet threw her head back and laughed. "Perfectly, although I think I just shocked your fiancée."

"We're fine," I said. "Thanks." I glanced at the time. "We'd better get back to campus. Don't you have a panel soon?"

Scarlet checked her watch. "You're right." She reached for her wallet, but Frank waved her away.

"This is my treat," he said.

"I'm going to run to the restroom, and then we'd better get back to campus." Scarlet grabbed her purse.

Frank pointed her toward the ladies' room.

When she was out of earshot, he leaned down. "Are you okay? You look pale."

"I'm fine. I was just surprised. She was really candid, and I didn't expect it."

"I don't think you should get in the car with her."

"I'll be fine. She's not angry with me. It's Judith Hunter who should never get within choking distance of her."

Frank reminded me, "She was close enough to her to have slipped something in her drink."

Scarlet returned.

I took the bag with Nana Jo and the twins' lunches, and we hurried back to the bookstore.

The ride back to campus was quick and quiet. I found a parking space close to the door and pulled in. On the walk back, Scarlet turned to me and said, "Look, I'll admit that I hate Judith Hunter, and I wouldn't shed a tear if someone poisoned her. In fact, I'd gladly dance naked on her grave. But I didn't do it."

Scarlet marched off to her panel discussion, leaving me staring after her. I needed to think. I still had an hour before my discussion on publishing. I went to my table and pulled out my laptop. Writing always helped me think, so I allowed my mind to drift to a different place and time.

Wickfield Lodge, Drawing Room

Dinner went off without a hitch, and Lady Elizabeth Marsh made a mental note to thank Mrs. Anderson. Each and every course was more delicious than the last. The guests lavished so much praise on the cook that Mrs. Anderson, who had been called up from the kitchen, actually blushed. Even Lady Dallyripple choked out a compliment. Everything had gone smoothly. Lady Elizabeth would need to find some way to reward all of the servants. Perhaps an extra day out?

After dinner, Lady Elizabeth led the women to the drawing room, leaving the men to drink port and smoke in the dining room. Lady Elizabeth sat in a comfortable chair nearest the fireplace and waited, her knitting on her lap. She and Penelope made casual conversation with Mrs. Baker, while Lady Dallyripple paced.

Lady Elizabeth encouraged her husband to be quick, so it was no surprise when the men quickly joined them in the drawing room and Colonel Livingston prepared to read from his book.

Lady Elizabeth exchanged a glance with her husband, who merely shrugged. Colonel Livingston was more than a little tipsy, and she was unsure of his ability to stand, let alone read.

"Colonel, perhaps you'd like to sit for a bit and have a strong cup of tea before—"

"Nonsense." Colonel Livingston waved away Lady Elizabeth's protest.

"I, for one, cannot wait to hear Colonel Livingston regale us with his own words," Lady Dallyripple said. She perched on the end of her seat and stared adoringly at the colonel.

The guests took their seats around the room and waited. Lady Elizabeth intercepted a look between Victor and James. Victor took a seat front and center.

"Indeed," Victor said. "I'm sure the colonel will have us all enthralled with tales of war and military life."

Oliver Birdwhistle and Sir Greyson Bythesea didn't seem as enthusiastic, but both men took their seats and waited.

Everyone focused their attention on Colonel Livingston.

Sebastian Lloyd assisted in getting the manuscript set up. Colonel Livingston dropped his glasses and then a handkerchief. The secretary picked them up and attempted to adjust the colonel's tie, which had gotten twisted over the course of the evening.

Colonel Livingston swatted away his assistant's hand. "Would you stop fussing."

The secretary complied, leaving the colonel red-faced and teetering. "Colonel, perhaps a cup of tea would be—"

"For the last time, I don't want a bloody cup of tea!" Colonel Livingston shouted. "If you want to be helpful, get me a glass of wine."

"Colonel!" Lord William said. "There are ladies present."

The colonel frowned but was careful of his language.

"Mr. Lloyd, sit here," Lady Dallyripple said, patting the seat next to her. "I'm sure I shall need a strong man to hold on to when the colonel's words transport us into the very heart of war. Lions, tigers, and elephants. Not to mention the natives. I just can't wait."

Lady Elizabeth bit her tongue to keep from telling Lady Dallyripple what she thought of her and her politics. The Marshes were patriotic and had served their nation faithfully for countless generations, but the colonization of other nations wasn't something Lady Elizabeth supported. Just as British citizens deserved to live in peace in their own nation, so too did the native inhabitants of India, Africa, and everywhere. However, this wasn't the time or the place to open that can of worms. Instead, she pulled out her knitting and attacked the baby blanket she was making.

Sebastian Lloyd took one last look at the colonel, who shooed the assistant away, before he took his position next to Lady Dallyripple.

The group waited for the reading to begin.

Glasses in place. Notes open. Colonel Livingston began reading.

Lady Elizabeth noted that unlike the other members of the dinner party, Lord Browning stood near the door. Not long after the reading began, he snuck out.

Colonel Livingston spent an excruciating amount of time recounting details of military life in the East African nation of Kenya.

Having traveled extensively in her younger days,

Lady Elizabeth had fond memories of the Colony and Protectorate of Kenya, or what her fellow Brits referred to as British East Africa. She remembered the diverse landscape with the savage beauty of the savanna. The dry, dusty desert, tropical white sand beaches on the Indian Ocean, and lush forests and mountains. Lady Elizabeth had literally gasped the first time she'd seen a giraffe in the wild.

Colonel Livingston didn't talk of the country's beauty, kindhearted people, or mineral-rich resources. He spoke of insects, poor roads and infrastructure, and drought. It seemed that Colonel Livingston disliked everything about the country.

Lady Elizabeth knitted and allowed her mind to wander. She wondered where her nephew had slipped off to and what he was doing. She allowed her mind to drift between Colonel Livingston's droning, monotonous ramblings back to the beautiful country she remembered.

After what felt like hours, Colonel Livingston moved away from describing terrain to describing missions. He went into detail, naming collaborators, code words used by the military, and even the inner workings of the military.

Lady Elizabeth wasn't the only person who found Colonel Livingston's book offensive. Based on the way Lord William bit the stem of his pipe and Lord Victor Carlston tugged at his ear, both men were uncomfortable. The tips of Sir Greyson Bythesea's ears were red, and Oliver Birdwhistle looked as though his buttons would explode.

Eventually, the tension in the room grew too much. Sir Greyson hopped up suddenly, and a small table nearby tumbled over. "Why, you . . . traitor."

"Sir Greyson," Lord William said.

Bythesea lunged toward the colonel, but Victor was up quickly and positioned himself between the colonel and the angry member of the House of Commons.

Oliver Birdwhistle stood. "You can't possibly mean to publish those lies."

Victor was grateful when Sebastian Lloyd moved in front of the colonel, allowing Victor to focus on preventing Birdwhistle from launching an assault.

However Lady Elizabeth expected Colonel Livingston to respond, laughter wasn't it. Nevertheless, that's exactly what he did. Colonel Basil Livingston tossed back his head and laughed.

"What's wrong, Birdwhistle?" Colonel Livingston said when he finally managed to talk. "Scared of the truth?"

"Truth? That's nothing but scandalous lies."

"The lies aren't the worst part of all that boring drivel," Sir Greyson said, his face purple with rage. "It's the details. My God, man. You can't possibly be serious about printing that. Not now, with the Nazis ready to invade our shores at any moment."

Lady Dallyripple tugged on his arm. "Sir Greyson, perhaps you should sit down. You need to be mindful about your blood pressure."

"How dare you," Birdwhistle said. "You've practically given Hitler a roadmap right into the very heart of Britain. Code words and special names and addresses of sympathizers. My God. You've opened the door and invited the enemy right in. You might as well send the Nazis a key to 10 Downing Street."

"Surely, you've changed the names to protect the real people," Penelope said. "This is fiction, right?"

"Why should I change the names?" Colonel Livingston said. "War is real. I've spent most of my life in the military, and there's only one conclusion that anyone with even half of an active brain cell can come to. War needs to stop. It's a no-win proposition. Therefore, the only way we can stop nations from sending countless men to their deaths is to level the playing field by opening all of the windows and doors and exposing everything to the light."

The Members of Parliament sputtered and protested.

Lady Elizabeth gazed at the colonel. "I agree that war is terrible. The devastation and loss of life is horrible, but it seems to me that you aren't leveling the playing field. You're exposing Britain's secrets and giving the Nazis an unfair advantage."

Colonel Livingston shrugged. "Perhaps if Britain feels she is superior, she should keep her nose out of what doesn't concern her. Besides, I have been assured that there are others who believe as I do. Once my book is made public, others will follow. Like-minded people in Germany, Poland, and even the United States will do the same. Then, governments will have no choice but to stop warmongering. They'll be forced to seek diplomatic solutions to problems as opposed to resorting to threats."

"Why, you traitorous simpleton," Birdwhistle said.

Sir Greyson Bythesea lunged toward Colonel Livingston.

Sebastian Lloyd pushed him backward, and Bythesea tripped over the table he'd previously knocked over.

Victor maintained a firm position between Birdwhistle and the colonel.

Penelope moved to the wall and pressed the buzzer. Thompkins arrived and assessed the situation. He hurried to the wall and pressed the buzzer again. Within moments, Frank and Jim joined Thompkins.

Frank MacTavish was young and strong. The number-one prop on the village rugby team, he easily had Sir Greyson Bythesea wrapped up in no time.

Sebastian Lloyd swung at Oliver Birdwhistle and punched him in the jaw.

Smaller than Frank, Jim was better known for his ability with a cricket bat, but as the rugby team's hooker, he was no slouch in a fight. He braced himself, leaned forward, and rammed his head into Sebastian Lloyd's abdomen.

Victor barely missed a swing by Oliver Birdwhistle but managed to slide the MP's jacket down, trapping his arms.

Lord Browning arrived in time to provide a firm grasp on Colonel Livingston's arm. "Alright, that's enough. Outside."

Thompkins rushed to hold the door while Frank, Jim, James, and Victor escorted the rowdy men outside.

Reverend Baker and Lord William Marsh had taken up positions to protect the women. The men corralled the women to the back corner of the room and away from the fray.

After the last of the fighters left, silence descended over the room. Lady Dallyripple went into hysterics.

"Lord-a-mercy, I've never seen such behavior," she wailed. "How in the world? Fisticuffs? Members of Parliament actually attacked a fine, upstanding man like Colonel Livingston."

Lady Elizabeth and Lady Penelope exchanged a look. However, it was Mrs. Baker who spoke.

"Amelia Dallyripple, you cannot possibly be condoning the part that Colonel Livingston played in that . . . unseemly display."

Mrs. Baker wasn't a member of the aristocracy, but her role as the wife of the village's spiritual leader carried weight in the small community.

"I was only . . . I was intending to imply that Basil could have been a bit more circumspect given the situation," Lady Dallyripple said.

Mrs. Baker turned to Lady Elizabeth. "I'm terribly sorry. None of this should have happened, and I hope that each of those men will apologize."

Lady Elizabeth assessed the condition of the drawing room, amazed that nothing was broken. "Thank you, but I suspect we haven't heard the last of this."

"What do you mean?" Lady Penelope asked.

"Oliver Birdwhistle and Sir Greyson Bythesea are conservatives who have supported Prime Minister Chamberlain's policy of appeasement. Neither of them have been in favor of war with Germany. However, they are both patriots. If this is an example of how conservatives react to Colonel Livingston's radical views, then heaven help us."

Chapter 22

I was shocked back to the present when the alarm I had set so I wouldn't be late to my discussion went off. One glance at the time, and I quickly saved my work and put my laptop away.

The discussion between traditional vs. indie publishing was surprisingly well attended. There were ten authors total. Five traditionally published authors seated at a long conference table on one side of the moderator, while four indie published authors sat on the other side of the moderator. One seat was empty. The program book confirmed that the seat was for Nora Cooper.

In the program book, the panel was billed as a debate. However, the reality was that an author's choice to publish traditionally or indie was a personal decision. There were pros and cons on both sides, and no definitive right or wrong. The indie authors argued for the desire to maintain autonomy over their work, as they controlled the content, illustrations, price, and every facet of their brands, while the traditional authors agreed that they were willing to give up both autonomy and money in exchange for the resources and distribution channels available to publishing houses. Based on the questions from the audience, there were quite a few aspiring authors present. Several mentioned social media ads claiming that authors could make seven-figure incomes self-publishing their books *if* they bought a heavily discounted *How To* course.

There was a time when I considered indie publishing my book, but I was too insecure to step out on my own. Nana Jo would have called that another example of my imposter syndrome. Writing a book was hard. Even for a former English teacher, there were times when I spent hours trying to find the perfect word or researching details about 1939 England. I wanted my book to be perfect. Yet, here it was. Finally in print, and after five revisions and a multitude of edits, I still found a typo. I can't imagine the hours of anguish I'd spend on cover illustrations and all of the other details that go into making a book. No, I wasn't cut out for indie publishing, but I had nothing but the highest respect for writers who do.

When the panel was over, I hurried to my table. There were two people who purchased my book and wanted a signature. Two people who wanted to know my opinion of my publisher. And one person who wanted me to recommend her to my agent.

I was thankful the banquet was moved to Saturday night. I was exhausted and in no mood to get dressed up again. I wanted nothing more than to go home and curl up with Snickers and Oreo and possibly one of their namesakes. I smiled.

"What's put that smile on your face?" Dorothy Clark asked.

"I was just thinking how nice it will be to go home and rest tonight."

Dorothy was shaking her head before the words left my mouth. "Haven't you checked your messages? Josephine sent a text to meet at Frank's for dinner and debrief."

"Ugh." I dropped my head onto the table.

Dorothy patted me on the back. "You probably have time for a power nap. You'll feel much better once you've slept."

I refused to admit how excited the idea of a power nap sounded. "I don't think I have time. I want to swing by the infirmary to check on Nora Cooper."

"Then we better get moving." Dorothy practically lifted me out of the chair. Was I embarrassed that my grandmother's seventy-year-old friend was both physically and mentally stronger than me? Not in the least.

We walked next door to the infirmary. A drill sergeant dressed like a nurse was manning the reception desk, but she wasn't very receptive.

"We'd like to see Nora Cooper."

"Who are you?"

"My name's Samantha Washington, and this—"

"No. Who are you to Miss Cooper?"

"We're friends." I stretched the truth a bit, but we were probably the closest thing that she had to friends at the book festival.

"No."

"Okay, we haven't known her long, but—"

"Immediate family members only."

"Can you tell us how she's doing?"

"No. That's confidential."

"We're not asking for her full medical history. We just want to know if she's okay. I brought her here earlier."

"Sorry. Those are the rules."

I thought about appealing to her compassion, but I felt sure she didn't have any.

Dorothy must have noticed that I was revving up for another round. "Come on, Sam." She grabbed me by the arm. Just as we were about to leave, she turned back to the drill sergeant and stopped. She saluted. Clicked her heels. "*Mon capitaine.*" She turned and marched out.

In the car, Dorothy said that Detective Pitt had assigned Officer Martinez to watch Judith Hunter for the remainder of the night. She asked me to drop her off at Shady Acres, which I did. She promised to meet us at Frank's later but said she wanted to get a start on her article about Judith Hunter for her nephew's magazine. Dorothy was excited about rekindling her journalistic skills, and I was thrilled.

At the bookstore, most of the customers who had crowded the store earlier were gone. There were just a few of my regulars left.

I opened the door that led upstairs, and Snickers and Oreo bounded down the stairs and outside to take care of business.

From the door, I couldn't help but notice how gray Snicers's muzzle was. She was close to fifteen, which was old in dog years, even little dog years. I used to believe that one year in human years was seven in dog years until my vet explained that smaller dogs lived longer and didn't age quite as rapidly as larger dogs. Dr. Britain explained that scientists now believe that a small dog ages about fifteen years in their first human year. Nine years in their second year. After that, a small dog ages roughly five years for each human year. Regardless of the math, fourteen in human years was still at least seventy-two in small-dog years. Pretty old for my toy poodle.

On a daily basis, I barely noticed the subtle changes. However, when I stopped and looked at pictures of her as a pup, I could see the signs of aging. When she was young, Snickers had been an energetic fireball. Now, she preferred sleeping rather than playing with toys or her brother. She preferred to walk instead of run. Plus, I'd noticed that her hearing wasn't quite as acute as it once had been. She'd been diagnosed with congestive heart failure, which probably played a part in the aging process. Nevertheless, she was still my girl, and I refused to think of life without her.

Oreo was only two years younger than Snickers, but he

was still as goofy as ever. He bounded out into the yard and pounced on a leaf. He tossed the leaf in the air and then barked as it blew across the yard.

Snickers and I watched him playing from the doorway. After a few moments, he remembered why he was out there. He ran to the side of the garage, hiked his leg, and then ran back inside.

Christopher and Zaq had dates, so I paid them handsomely for the assistance today and gave them both some extra pocket money. Both twins made more than I had teaching in the public school system, so money wasn't the reason they helped me at the bookstore. That just made me want to give them even more.

I offered to take over and give Nana Jo a break, which she took. I loved working in the bookshop. Just walking inside had the power to energize and invigorate me. Books were my happy place. Surrounded by books, I felt safe. I helped a couple find two new thrillers. I spent time chatting with one of my regular patrons, Kay Lillie. She was a voracious reader. The fact that she loved my book endeared her to me even more.

When the last person left, I spent a few minutes tidying up. The box of Nora Cooper's books was still full. However, there were just a handful of books left for Scarlet MacDunkin and none for Paul West or Olivia Townsend. Before I dropped Dorothy off, she said that Judith Hunter had promised to do a signing Saturday morning.

By the time the store was closed up, cleaned, and ready for the next day, it was time for dinner. Nana Jo came down, and we walked over to Frank's.

We went upstairs, where Jenna and the girls were waiting for us.

Nana Jo took her seat at the head of the table. Our waiter was new. He had a bright smile and looked barely old enough to be driving, let alone taking alcoholic beverage orders. However, he was soft spoken and kind. He barely batted an eye when Irma flirted with him. Frank must have warned him never to turn his back to her because he went to great lengths to avoid having his fanny anywhere close enough to pinch.

We waited until we'd finished eating to discuss business. As soon as the meal was completed, Nana Jo pulled out her iPad. She tapped her stylus against her glass and called for order.

I kicked things off by sharing what I'd learned from Judith Hunter about Nora Cooper and what I'd learned from Scarlet MacDunkin.

Frank whistled. "That's some friend."

"Judith Hunter sounds like she could teach classes on backstabbing and treachery," Nana Jo said. "At least Judas Iscariot got thirty pieces of silver for betraying Jesus. From the sound of it, Judith Hunter betrayed Scarlet for the joy of bringing down a . . . dare I call it, friend? What on earth could she get out of that?"

"Beats me," Dorothy said. "But remind me never to turn my back on that one." She shuddered.

I turned to Jenna. "Would that contract that Judith got Nora to sign be legal?"

"I doubt it. It depends on a lot of factors. What type of facility was it? Was it just a hospital? Or was it a mental hospital? If she was committed to a mental hospital, she might not have been mentally competent to go into a legal contract."

"I'll bet that's part of what Nora Cooper discovered," Nana Jo said. "I'll bet she remembered writing the book. Maybe she reached out to Clark, who, now that he was clean from the drugs and his brain was working again, remembered the manuscript."

"Did someone have power of attorney?" Jenna asked.

"Judith didn't say," I said.

Jenna frowned.

"What?"

"Nothing. It just sounds really . . . smarmy. I mean, if Judith's father ran the facility, he might have been given power of attorney. Or he could have appointed a lawyer to represent Nora, but not all lawyers are created equal. Plus, she may not have been committed. She may have just been staying there for a rest, in which case competence might be difficult to prove." Jenna shook her head. "The law is hard."

We spent a few minutes hashing and rehashing Nora's mental state but didn't get much further than we had earlier. "I might as well keep going," Jenna said. "This clarifies and muddies the water from what we were talking about earlier. If Judith had a contract showing that she bought the manuscript, then the issue becomes whether or not Nora Cooper was mentally competent to enter into a contract. Given Nora's behavior and the fact that she's currently at a hospital, this will certainly make the legal aspects of the case more interesting."

"Who wants to go next?" Nana Jo asked.

Ruby Mae raised her hand. "I had a good talk with Donovan, my cousin's grandson." She pulled her knitting out from the bag she carried with her and began to knit as she spoke.

"Donovan didn't know anything about Dr. Leonard Peters, other than he's a media hound. Mrs. Graves is an interesting person. Apparently, she is a super wealthy alum and board member. Some of the students call her the Mafia Boss or Godmother. Of course, they only say it behind her back."

"What does she do?" I asked.

"No one really knows. According to Donovan, she just showed up on campus a few years ago. She got an office, and the title on the door says Director, but no one knows of what." Ruby Mae paused to count stitches and then continued. "Anyway, she rules the book festival committee with an iron fist and has connections in high places."

"It's probably the money," Dorothy said. "If she's wealthy, the university will bow to her in the hopes that she'll leave them a huge legacy in her will." She should know. Dorothy's late husband owned a string of dry cleaners, and when he died, he left her pretty well cared for, although she never flaunted her wealth unless the situation called for it.

"Anyone else want to report?" Nana Jo asked.

Irma took a deep breath. "I didn't learn anything about Leonard Peters. I think he's gay."

"Because he didn't fawn over you?"

"So, what if he is?" Dorothy said. "What's that got to do with anything?"

"I wasn't able to get anything out of him, that's what," Irma said. "I all but threw myself at him." She glanced around the table looking for sympathy. She didn't find any.

Dorothy rolled her eyes.

Ruby Mae shook her head and focused on her knitting.

Jenna looked ready to burst out laughing and quickly took a sip of Moscato to hide her face.

Nana Jo squinted and leaned toward Irma. "First off, just because a man doesn't fall for a dish that's being shoved in his face doesn't mean he's gay. Second, Dorothy's right. So what if he's gay? Your task is to get information."

"I've always been able to get men to open up to me." Irma patted her beehive hairdo and pulled out a compact to check her makeup.

"Jesus, take the wheel," Nana Jo said.

"After dinner, I'm going out with Smithy. I *know* he'll talk. I'll get the scoop." She turned to me. "Don't you worry, Sam. I'll pull my weight."

I reached across and patted her hand. "I know you will, Irma. You always do."

"That's right. I do, don't I?" She sat up straighter. "I'll get that son of a bi—"

"Irma!"

Irma burst into a coughing fit. "Sorry."

Frank made multiple trips up and down the stairs through-out the meal. He raised his hand. "If it's okay, I don't have a lot of time, so I'd like to go next."

Everyone nodded their agreement.

"My job was to look into Nora Cooper's and Judith Hunter's financial situations. I went ahead and gave my friend the names of all of the key players." He pulled a piece of paper from his pocket and read. "Scarlet MacDunkin's in financial trouble. Nora Cooper makes enough to keep a roof over her head. Judith Hunter is the wealthiest. Her book has been selling well, but prior to that she was well off. Her grandfather was a writer, Alex Savage. He—"

"Wait!" I said. "Judith Hunter's grandfather was fantasy writer Alex Savage?"

"I guess it's the same guy. My friend didn't mention what he wrote."

"Alex Savage is a legend. I love his books."

"Me too," Nana Jo said. "He wrote science fiction and fantasy. I loved his books. I haven't seen anything from him in years. I wonder what happened to him." Nana Jo started swiping her phone. She paused to read, but then she shook her head. "Nothing. I'm not seeing anything about why he stopped writing or when another book is coming out."

"Maybe he died," Irma said.

"I sure hope not," I said. "I mean, he was so good."

Nana Jo put down her phone. "Nothing online to indicate he's not alive and kicking."

"I wonder why he stopped writing?"

Frank shrugged. "I can ask my friend if you want."

"No. I mean, it probably isn't a key factor in Clark Cunningham's murder." I appreciated Frank's connections. They came in handy when we were investigating a murder, but I certainly didn't want to press my luck by asking him to look into something that was just idle curiosity. "I can't believe Judith Hunter's his granddaughter. Maybe that's where she got the idea to become a writer."

"Anyway, her grandfather set up a trust for her," Frank said. "The bottom line is she has money. She made even more with her book, and while she hasn't gotten the money from selling the film rights, yet—at least it hasn't been deposited into her bank account—when she does get the money, she won't have to write another book if she doesn't want to."

"Anything else?"

"Paul West struggled for several years. His most recent book is doing well. His wife makes more on her middle-grade mysteries. The only suspicious thing about any of their finances was that Clark Cunningham was getting quite a bit of money from Judith Hunter, but he was her publicist. So, I'm sure she had to pay him a fee."

"True," Nana Jo said. "I've seen her name everywhere. You can't walk five feet without seeing a picture of her book on the side of a bus, in magazines, everywhere."

"I went to visit my granddaughter, Jillian, last month," Dorothy said. "We went to Times Square, and lo and behold, there she was."

"Wow," I said. "That had to cost a small fortune."

Nana Jo looked down the table at Dorothy, who seemed to be in her own world. "I'll go next if there are no objections."

No one objected.

"Freddie's son, Mark, ran the names through the state police database but didn't learn anything we haven't already found out. Paul West and Olivia Townsend came to sign stock. That man was slicker than a greased hog at a hog wrestling contest."

Sometimes, I forgot my grandmother grew up on a farm

until she came up with one of her unusual idioms. "What's hog wrestling?"

"You grease a hog, and then four people have to catch it and stuff it into a barrel in four minutes."

"Sounds cruel."

"Lots of folk agree with you. It's illegal in Minnesota. There's a movement to get it banned." She shook her head. "I suppose it is terrifying for the hogs, but back when I was young, folks didn't think too much about how animals felt. Anyway, my point is that Paul West flashed his smile, flirted with the women, signed books, and put on a great show. When he wasn't showing off for his fans, he trash-talked Judith Hunter to me and anyone who would listen."

"Oh no." I rubbed my forehead. "Please tell me you're joking."

"Nope. Not joking. That man has an axe to grind, and he was willing to grind it all day long. Finally, I put my foot down. I told him that we don't trash other authors here." Nana Jo looked at me, and I mouthed my thanks.

"He sounds like a real jacka—"

"Irma!"

"What was his wife doing while he did this?" Jenna asked.

"You mean the life-sized Barbie doll?" Nana Jo said. "She was so busy fluttering her false eyelashes and staring adoringly at her husband that I don't think she heard one word of it." She stuck her finger down her throat. "I wanted to smack her upside her head and knock some sense into her, but I was afraid I might throw off her center of balance."

Jenna choked on her wine, and I had to smack her back.

"So, she's had some . . . enhancements?" Ruby Mae asked.

"Let's just say, if we were both on the *Titanic*, I would have held on to her to stay afloat," Nana Jo said.

"Nana Jo!" My grandmother was always supportive of

women. I was surprised to hear her criticize a woman's body choices.

"Look, I don't care what people want to do to make themselves happy. Surgery, tattoos, whatever. Women own their bodies and have the right to do whatever they want. I support those choices as long as they do them for the right reason. If you don't like your nose, change it. You want a bigger bust, lips, butt? Do whatever makes you happy. I'll fight to the death for your right to own your body. However, if you're changing yourself to try to please someone else, well . . . I think you're headed for disappointment."

"There's a picture of her in one of her first books," I said. "She was always a beautiful woman. When Paul got involved with Judith Hunter, she was devastated. When their affair finally ended, and he came home, she must have felt like she needed to do something. At least, that's the impression I got from our conversation earlier."

"In that case, Josephine's right," Dorothy said. "She shouldn't have wasted her time or her money." She frowned.

"What do you mean?" I asked.

"It isn't over. Paul West and Judith Hunter are still having an affair."

Chapter 23

Dorothy's bombshell left me shell-shocked and staring at her with my mouth hanging open. "How do you know?"

"I spent most of the day trailing Judith Hunter. Most of the time, she was talking to fans. Signing books. Giving interviews. Posing for pictures. You know, all the stuff a famous author would do. At one point, she got up to take a picture with a fan, and she left her phone on the table. She got a text message, and I just happened to see it."

"What did it say?" Nana Jo asked.

"'Meet me in the stairwell.'"

"Who was it from?" I already knew the answer, but I asked anyway.

"*P.W.* is what appeared on the screen."

My mind didn't want to accept that Paul West had lied to his wife and was still involved with Judith Hunter. "Maybe it wasn't him. Maybe it was a different P.W."

Dorothy shook her head. "When Judith returned, she saw the message and excused herself. Of course, I followed her. I saw her slip into the stairwell. Before the door closed completely, I saw them. She and Paul West were kissing. Before you ask, it wasn't a brotherly kiss."

"But at the banquet, he acted as though he hated Judith," I said, and turned to Frank, who nodded his confirmation.

"*Acted* is the key, isn't it?" Nana Jo said.

"Poor Olivia," I said. "She's going to be so devastated."

"If I handled divorce," Jenna said, "I would volunteer my services and take him for every penny he has."

I glared at Frank. "Men who cheat make me so angry."

"Hold on," he said, holding up both hands. "Not all men cheat."

"I'm sorry. I didn't mean to include all men in that. I know that there are some good men who would never dream of cheating on their spouses." I smiled.

"Especially when the one they love writes murder mysteries and probably knows at least one hundred ways to commit murder."

"Like Olivia Townsend?" Nana Jo asked.

"If she knew, that would certainly give her a good reason for wanting to poison Judith Hunter," I said. I didn't want to believe that Olivia Townsend was the killer, but Nana Jo was right. If Paul West was still having an affair with Judith Hunter, and Olivia found out, that would certainly give her a good reason for murder.

Dorothy must have noticed the panicked look on my face. "Don't worry," she said. "I'm going to be watching out for her. She's staying at the inn on MISU's campus. I got a room near hers. I'll keep an eye on her. It'll be my first stakeout."

"Thank you, Dorothy, but this could be dangerous. I wouldn't want you to get hurt."

"Don't worry. I'll be fine. Besides, I've never been on a stakeout before. I think it'll be fun."

"Maybe I should go with you," Nana Jo said. "We can

work in shifts. That's the way the detectives do it in the P.I. novel I'm reading."

"Wait, I think this is going way too far," I said. "Maybe we need to leave this to the professionals. Detective Pitt had Officer Martinez watching her earlier. This could get dangerous, and besides, that's his job."

Nana Jo waved away my concerns. "Pshaw. We're not planning to chase down a gun-wielding felon. We're just going to be watching Judith Hunter. We'll make sure no one tries to slip something in her food or drink, and if we see anyone suspicious, we'll call Stinky Pitt immediately."

"I'm not sure about this." I glanced from Dorothy to Nana Jo. "I don't like the idea of the two of you on a stakeout."

"We'll be fine," Nana Jo said. "Besides, I'll bring my Peacemaker." She patted her purse.

The thought of my grandmother on a stakeout with a loaded gun was not in the least bit comforting. I argued a bit longer, but the two women had made up their minds. They were determined, and nothing I said was going to change them. However, they did swear to be careful, to not take unnecessary risks, and to phone for help if they saw anything suspicious.

"Sam, I know you're concerned, and I appreciate that," Nana Jo said. "But we are well able to take care of ourselves. Trust me."

Despite the gnawing concern in my stomach, I agreed.

We finished up and decided that we would skip meeting for breakfast. There wouldn't be much happening overnight. The banquet was tomorrow, so we would meet at the bookstore in the afternoon.

Frank and I said our goodbyes, and I walked back to the bookstore. My brain was racing with all of the details that I'd learned. I didn't feel any closer to figuring out who murdered

Clark Cunningham. Tomorrow was the last full day of the festival. The awards banquet had been rescheduled for Saturday night. Sunday morning, there would be a breakfast and a few panels. Then, by noon, everyone would pack up and go their separate ways. The killer would have gotten away with murder.

Dawson was in the kitchen baking, while Snickers and Oreo sat attentively waiting for him to drop something on the floor.

I was exhausted, but I knew I wouldn't be able to sleep. My brain was still too active. So, I sat down at my laptop.

Wickfield Lodge, Lawn

Lady Elizabeth Marsh and Lady Penelope Carlston strolled around the grounds of Wickfield Lodge. Lady Penelope pushed a pram that held the sleeping Lord William. The lawns were crammed full of people. Union flags, streamers, balloons, and brightly colored bunting waved in the wind and defined the various areas for games, food, and crafts. The tea tent took center stage. There was a buzz in the air.

"How is Mrs. Anderson holding up?" Lady Penelope asked. "She always went into overdrive before the fete when we were children."

"She's still a nervous wreck," Lady Elizabeth said. "I didn't even want to stick my head down there to wish her luck." She smiled. "I'm thinking she might be in need of a long holiday when this is over."

"Especially after last night."

"That was horrible. I can't believe they actually got into a brawl in our drawing room. I may never forgive Amelia for that."

"You think she orchestrated things?"

"I don't know." Lady Elizabeth frowned. "I can't believe she knew there would be an actual fight. She couldn't have known the men would resort to actually hitting one another, but she had to know that bringing people with such differing opinions together under one roof would result in calamity. Amelia and I don't share the same views where politics are concerned, but we have known each other for years, and she is a snob. I would hope that if she didn't respect me or our friendship that she would at the very least respect my connections enough that she wouldn't want to risk being ostracized from society simply to disrupt a dinner party. To what end?"

"Alice, our new daily, lives next door to Lionel Cuthbert," Lady Penelope said. "Alice said that the electrical isn't as bad as Lady Dallyripple says. She said there was no reason she couldn't have hosted that party last night. Everyone in the village thinks it was just an attempt to throw Mrs. Anderson off kilter and place her in a bad light with two of the judges right before the contest."

Lady Elizabeth sighed. "I certainly don't want to think ill of anyone, especially someone I've known for years, but I can't deny the thought did cross my mind."

"I'm glad it didn't work. Last night's dinner was amazing. How on earth did she manage to pull that off on such short notice?"

"Mrs. Anderson is a great cook, but last night took me by surprise as well. However, I suppose if nothing else, it distracted her so she wasn't able to focus on the contest today."

The two ladies made their way to the main stage in time to see Colonel Basil Livingston opening the fete. The colonel's eyes were bloodshot, and he had a red circle around his right eye that would be purple and then black within the next two days.

Lady Amelia Dallyripple, Reverend Baker, and Colonel Livingston stood atop the platform. Reverend Baker made a few brief announcements, then turned to Lady Amelia Dallyripple. In a lavender ensemble that included a matching new hat, Lady Dallyripple stepped forward and introduced Colonel Basil Livingston.

"She looks as though she's headed to Ascot in that getup," Lady Penelope whispered.

Lady Dallyripple gushed about the "world renowned, critically acclaimed author," whom she claimed was working on a book that would change the world.

"Laying it on a bit thick, isn't she?" Lord Browning said.

Lady Elizabeth hadn't noticed that Lord James Browning had joined them until he spoke.

Colonel Basil Livingston nodded to acknowledge the applause. Then he moved toward the microphone and declared the village fete officially open.

The crowd erupted in cheers and tumultuous applause, which was a notable contrast to the tepid response to the special guest. Lady Dallyripple frowned her disapproval, but then she caught sight of a reporter from the local newspaper taking photos and plastered a smile on her face.

The children whooped and ran toward their favorite games. The local orchestra started playing a foxtrot by Bram Martin and His Dance Orchestra, which had been popular with the younger set.

Lord Browning, Lady Elizabeth, and Lady Penelope painted a lovely picture of quaint village life as they strolled around the grounds with their pram.

"Where's Lord William?" Lord Browning asked. "I would have thought his lordship would have had to pose for pictures bobbing for apples or judging sheep."

"Sitting not very quietly with his leg propped up on a pillow," Lady Elizabeth said. "I warned him not to overindulge last night."

"Gout?"

Lady Elizabeth nodded. "I'm afraid Mrs. Anderson's delicious meal proved a bit too rich for him."

"Plus, there was the wine and port he had, to wash it all down," Lady Penelope added.

"Where's Victor?" Lord Browning asked. "Don't tell me he's been waylaid by fine food and drink too."

Lady Penelope waved her arm in the general vicinity of the sheep contest. "He's determined to win the fleece contest and has Dolly washed and combed and all dolled up."

"Dolly?" Lord Browning raised an eyebrow. "Don't tell me you've named the sheep?"

Lady Penelope stamped her foot. "Of course, I've named them, and once they've been named, they're a part of the family and *not* to be considered for lamb chops or roasted mutton."

"He should have warned me. One of the first things Daphne did was to name all of the animals." He grinned. "I wondered why my meals have had an abundance of fish and vegetables."

"I'm glad Reverend Baker convinced us to move forward with the fete," Lady Elizabeth said. "I'm glad to have this memory to take with me in the years to come." She glanced around and released a heavy sigh.

Lady Penelope stopped and put an arm around her aunt. "Now, don't get morbid, or I'll flop down on the ground and howl. I don't want to even think about Victor leaving to go . . ." She pulled a handkerchief from her sleeve and quickly wiped her eyes. "See what you started."

Little Lord William awoke from his nap and demanded attention with a large wail.

"Oh, fiddlesticks," Lady Penelope said. "He'll need a change."

Lady Elizabeth turned to accompany her, but Lady Penelope stopped her. "No need for both of us to miss all of the fun. You enjoy yourself. We'll be back."

Lady Elizabeth and Lord Browning continued their stroll, stopping to admire various items along the way.

Lady Elizabeth noted that her nephew seemed to be looking for something or someone. "Did you find what you were looking for last night?"

Lord Browning grinned. "I should have known I couldn't hide anything from you." He grew serious. "I searched Colonel Livingston's cottage, but I didn't find notes or anything that might jeopardize our nation, but I might have been too late."

"What do you mean?"

"Victor reported everything he heard, and based on what the colonel said and some concerning reports we're getting about German collaborators, any sensitive information he had may have already been passed along to German spies. We may be too late."

Lady Elizabeth was about to speak when she caught sight of something from the corner of her eye that caused her to stop and stare. "Isn't that Colonel Livingston?"

Lord Browning turned to look. "It certainly is. He seems to be having an argument. Any idea who that woman is?"

"Her face looks familiar, but I have no idea who she is. She's certainly not from around here. Not the way she's dressed." Lady Elizabeth stared at the woman. Suddenly, she snapped her fingers. "I know where I've seen her. She was in the *Times*. That's Eloise Fernsby."

"Should I recognize the name?" Lord Browning frowned.

"Not unless you read the society column." Lady Elizabeth smiled. "Eloise Fernsby is a famous publicist. She just got engaged to an American actor. You know, the one who plays in all of those cowboy movies. I forget his name."

"I wouldn't have taken you for the type for cowboy movies."

"I'm not, but William is. He just loves those films. Anyway, he's worth a small fortune, and I believe he's related to Mrs. Roosevelt."

The arguing couple were behind Wickfield Lodge in an area that had been cordoned off from the fete crowds.

"Follow me," Lady Elizabeth said, and she led James through a side door and around to a corner where they were within earshot of the fighting couple but still sheltered from view.

"Listen here, Eloise," Colonel Livingston said.

"You're supposed to be lining up big-ticket events. Not these dowdy little village fetes that don't pay a plug nickel."

"Look, I'm doing my best, but in case you hadn't noticed, the country's on the verge of war. Not a lot of people have the stomach to listen to a batty old colonel prattle on about the Great War when we're about to go through the same bloody madness again."

Colonel Livingston's face turned as red as the bruise around his eye. "Well, I hope you don't expect me to continue paying you. If you were as concerned about your clients as you've been in chasing after that no-talent hack of an actor, you might have been able to do your job."

"Oh no you don't. You owe me. I had to pay out of my own pocket to get anyone to even listen to you, let alone book you to speak. I had to foot the money for those photos of you at Cambridge and walking through the War Office. You owe me, and I'll get what's owed me one way or the other."

Despite the secluded location, their raised voices started to attract attention from nearby crowds.

Sebastian Lloyd hurried over to the arguing couple. "*Stoppen*," he whispered to Colonel Livingston.

From the angle where Lady Elizabeth stood, she had a clear view of Colonel Livingston's face. His eyes bulged, and a vein on the side of his neck pulsed as though it was ready to explode. However, within seconds, the wave passed, and his face changed from purple to red and then quickly faded back to its normal hue. The only sign of his momentary furor was the vein on the side of his neck.

Lloyd glanced around and noticed the crowd staring in their direction. He forced a smile that never reached his eyes. "You're late for judging the baking contest." He turned to Eloise Fernsby. "Please excuse us."

Sebastian Lloyd ushered the colonel away. With no show to watch, the crowd returned to their activities.

Eloise Fernsby glared at Colonel Livingston's retreating back for several moments and then marched away.

Lady Elizabeth turned to her nephew. "Was that German?"

Lord Browning nodded. "Indeed it was."

"I could only make out parts of what he said. Could you hear him?"

"He said, 'Pull yourself together, or I'll make sure this makes it into my next report.'"

They followed Lloyd and Colonel Livingston to the baking contest and observed while he, Birdwhistle, and Bythesea judged. There was a coolness between the three men, but any signs of the hatred that had led to a fistfight were kept under control.

The three men tasted all of the entries. The Marshes' cook, Mrs. Anderson, was the last entry.

The judges tasted and quickly jotted down their ratings on the cards next to their plates.

Mrs. Baker approached and took the cards. After a quick review with the judges, she handed them the blue ribbon and turned to face the crowd.

"This year's winner of the village baking contest is . . ." She paused for dramatic effect. "Mrs. Anderson."

The crowd erupted in applause.

Lady Elizabeth glanced at Lady Dallyripple, who stood near a tall man dressed in a white double-breasted chef's coat, a tall pleated white hat, and black-and-white houndstooth pants. Lady Dallyripple was furious and glared at the chef, who graciously walked over to congratulate Mrs. Anderson on her win.

The reporters who snapped photos earlier took several of Mrs. Anderson standing with the judges and holding the large blue ribbon.

Lady Elizabeth smiled when she saw the look of pride on Mrs. Anderson's face. When the pictures were over, she quickly hurried over to congratulate her.

Sebastian Lloyd pushed a cart with small plates of cake and cups of tea. Lloyd handed cups to Bythesea and Birdwhistle and then got a cup from the cart and passed it to Colonel Livingston.

Livingston stumbled into Lloyd, causing him to spill his tea.

"I'm terribly sorry, old boy. Here, take mine." Colonel Livingston passed his tea to his secretary.

Lloyd picked up a plate and took a bite of cake. "Mmm. This is delicious." He quickly ate the remainder of the cake. He wiped his mouth and then picked up his cup. He sipped the tea. He took several sips but then suddenly stopped. He dropped the cup and clawed at his collar. Within moments, he dropped to the ground and convulsed.

Lady Amelia Dallyripple screamed.

Lord Browning and Lady Elizabeth rushed to Lloyd's side.

"Someone call Doctor Haygood," Mrs. Baker yelled.

Lady Elizabeth looked up. "It's too late. He's dead."

Lady Dallyripple screamed again, and then she too dropped to the ground in a dead faint.

"I smell bitter almonds," Lady Elizabeth whispered to Lord Browning. "I think he's been poisoned."

Chapter 24

I spent a restless night dreaming of fetes, poison, and the pink plastic Barbie Dreamhouse I had as a kid. About two hours before my alarm was scheduled to go off, I was jolted awake by a loud noise. I sat bolt upright and glanced around in an attempt to get my bearings.

My phone vibrated, and my heart raced. No call at this time of the morning was ever good news.

I picked up the phone and took a few seconds to glance at the caller's name. The momentary relief I felt at not seeing my mom or a member of my family's face was short-lived. No picture. Only initials. When I realized the B.P. initials belonged to Detective Bradley Pitt, my heart rate increased to the beat of a fox-trot.

"Hello."

"Somebody just made another attempt on Judith Hunter's life."

"Judith Hunter?" My brain processed a lot of information in fractions of a nanosecond. First, Judith Hunter wasn't related to me. *Breathe*. Second, he said *attempt*. That meant the attempt failed. Third, a failed attempt meant still alive. *Breathe*.

Fourth, why was Detective Pitt calling me? "I don't under-stand, why—" That's when it hit me. "Nana Jo?"

"Your grandmother's fine," Detective Pitt said without his usual snideness, but there was a pregnant pause.

"Dorothy?" I gasped.

"Mrs. Clark was injured while—"

"Give me that phone," Nana Jo said in the background. She must have taken the phone away from Detective Pitt be-cause there was what sounded like tussling. After a moment, her voice came clearly through his phone. "Sam, Dorothy's fine. She lost her mind and thought she was Wonder Woman. Tried to leap over a bench and fell and twisted her ankle. The dang fool is lucky she didn't break her neck."

"Thank God."

"It's Nora Cooper. She attacked Judith Hunter."

"Nora? I thought she was in the hospital."

"Not anymore. Right now, she's lying in a bloody heap at the bottom of the bluffs."

Chapter 25

I don't remember getting dressed or driving to MISU's campus, but I did. Every police, fire, and emergency vehicle in Berrien County was on the campus with their lights flashing.

MISU didn't have a lot of dorms, but most of the students were standing behind the yellow crime scene tape watching when I screeched to a halt.

I leapt out of the car and ran toward the tape.

A policeman yelled for me to stop.

"Officer, my grandmother's back there. She called, and Detective Pitt said it was okay for me to come. Get him on the radio. He'll tell you."

The officer gave me a cynical look. But I didn't know him, so maybe that was the way he always looked. He stared at me for several beats as though he were waiting for me to change my story and confess that my ultimate goal in getting behind that crime scene tape was to single-handedly destroy evidence. I didn't flinch. I taught English to high school students who could smell fear a mile away. Woe to the teacher stupid enough to blink during a stare-down. But he was good.

Really good. He let nearly an entire minute pass before he reached for his radio.

Cleared to pass, I ducked under the tape and hurried across the lawn toward Lake Michigan.

MISU's campus sat on the Lake Michigan coastline. In the summer, it provided a tranquil backdrop for the campus. The campus wasn't on the beach. It sat on a bluff that looked out over the lake. Thousands of years ago, ice glaciers reached all the way to where the MISU campus now stood. But time, climate change, and a host of other environmental factors meant that Lake Michigan's coastline was eroding at about a foot annually. The university fenced off the area to keep students from trying to climb down the sandy cliffs to the boulders below and then onto the beach. Still, the fence didn't deter foolhardy students intent on taking risks. The ones who lived to tell their tales were often left paralyzed or with permanent injuries after the sandy soil collapsed underfoot, crashing them down onto the razor-sharp rocks.

Nana Jo waved to draw my attention. "Sam, over here."

I ran toward her and flung myself in her arms. "I'm so glad you're okay."

"I'm fine. It's Super Girl you need to be concerned about." She pointed to a bench where Dorothy Clark sat.

"Dorothy, are you okay? I'm so sorry. I—"

"I'm fine. It's just a sprain, which is what I keep telling them. I do *not* need medical attention."

"Dorothy, you need to go to the hospital and let them take X-rays," I said. "You can never be too safe."

"I'll go to the hospital. But I'll go on my own terms. I'm not going out on that thing until I'm good and dead." She pointed to the gurney the EMTs had wheeled down.

"Stubborn as a mule," Nana Jo murmured loud enough for Dorothy to hear.

"Takes one to know one," Dorothy fired back.

If the banter was anything to go by, Dorothy and Nana Jo were both fine, which eased my stress. I took a deep breath.

"They've been arguing like that ever since I got here," Detective Pitt said upon joining our group. He was followed by Judith Hunter, who was wrapped in a blanket and looked as though she were two seconds away from shock.

I pointed to the stretcher. "Judith, maybe you should lie down."

"Don't you start on me too," Judith snapped. "I just spent the last fifteen minutes convincing Detective Pitt, four EMTs, and the medical examiner that I do *not* need to go to the hospital. I'm fine."

"Well, you don't look fine," Nana Jo said. "You look like you're in shock."

"I'm fine. I just need to get away from here. I need a strong drink." She stood up and turned to Detective Pitt. "Am I under arrest?"

"No."

"Good. Then, I'm going inside. If you have any more questions, I'll be at the bar." She shrugged out of the blanket and marched toward the inn without looking back.

"Now that sounds like a good idea," Dorothy said and trudged after Judith. Her limp was barely noticeable.

Nana Jo and I exchanged glances and then followed after the retreating women.

The MISU bar was small, cozy, and warm, with wood-paneled walls and leather-seated booths. The atmosphere was more appealing to visiting parents and faculty than frat boys. It was Saturday morning, and last call had since come and gone, but the bartender was also the late-shift manager and was willing to accommodate a prestigious guest's request for a drink, no matter the time.

Judith and Dorothy were installed in a corner booth. Nana Jo and I slid in. A white-shirted waiter took our drink orders and then hurried to the bar to fill them.

Brandy was what they gave people in detective novels who had suffered a shock. We each ordered one.

Detective Pitt sauntered in, pulled up a chair, and sat down. He pointed at Judith, Nana Jo, and Dorothy. "Look, I need a statement from each of you. But let's start with you two."

Dorothy and Nana Jo exchanged a look, but then Nana Jo started. "We were worried about Judith."

"Me? Why on earth would either of you be worried about me?"

"Because the killer missed the first time," Dorothy said. "We thought he or she might try again."

"You're not really a reporter, are you?" Judith asked Dorothy.

"I am doing an article on you, but Sam asked me to keep an eye on you. She was worried. You can't tell from my performance tonight, but I have black belts in judo and aikido."

Judith smiled. "I thought there was something different about you."

"Alright. Alright," Detective Pitt said. "So, you were worried and decided to get a room at the inn to keep an eye on Miss Hunter. Then what happened?"

"Josephine and I took turns watching the door."

"Did anyone come by the room?" Pitt asked.

"No. It was dead quiet. Nothing happened. Not until around two, when Miss Hunter came out of her room and went down the hall. I woke up Josephine. She got her gun, and we took off after her."

At the mention of the gun, Detective Pitt stopped scribbling in his notepad and shot Nana Jo a curious look, but she cut off his question.

"I have a permit to carry, so just keep writing," Nana Jo said.

"We followed her out back along the bluffs, but we were behind," Dorothy said. "By the time we saw her, she was on the bluffs wrestling with someone."

"Nora Cooper," Nana Jo said. "That's who it was."

"It looked like Nora was trying to push Judith over the cliff," Dorothy said. "That's when I ran to help." She paused and pointed to her ankle, which was now propped on a chair. "That's when I tripped over the bench and sprained my ankle."

"I stopped to make sure Dorothy was okay, but then I headed to the bluff," Nana Jo said. "I would have shot Nora, but they were wrestling, and I couldn't risk hitting Judith by mistake."

Detective Pitt looked as though he wanted to make a smart comment about Nana Jo's shooting ability, but thankfully he thought better of it. He turned his attention to Judith. "What's your story?"

"I got a call from Nora. She said to meet her on the bluffs. She said if I met her, we could get to the bottom of this business about the manuscript once and for all." Judith stared at the brandy in her glass. "So, I went. I went to the bluffs, and there she was. She was waiting for me." She paused and took a long drink.

"What happened next?" Detective Pitt asked.

"She had a gun. She was going to kill me. We fought. I managed to get the gun away from her, and I tossed it over the bluffs. Then, she lunged at me. She was like a madwoman. She screamed and clawed at me. She was strong. So strong. I don't know how I managed to keep my balance, but I did. I guess my survival instincts kicked in." She shuddered. "Anyway, I somehow managed to get her off balance. I think she heard the two of you coming. She turned to look, and that's when I . . ."

I squeezed Judith's hand.

"It was horrible. She went over the bluffs and . . ." Judith took a long drink. After a few moments: "I don't know if I can ever unsee that. Every time I close my eyes, I just see her sprawled over the rocks."

"That's enough," Nana Jo said. "You're both going to the hospital." She pointed to Judith. "You need a tranquilizer." She turned to Dorothy. "You need to get that ankle wrapped and some good painkillers. Sam, bring the car around."

"I've got a report to fill out," Detective Pitt said. "I need—"

"You need to stop wearing plaid with polka dots," Nana Jo said.

Detective Pitt glanced down at his pink and green polka-dot shirt and his orange and yellow plaid polyester pants. "What's wrong with—"

"Detective Pitt, we're tired," Nana Jo said. "Your case is closed. Whatever you need to ask can wait. You have your killer. Now, we need to move on with our lives."

Chapter 26

North Harbor was a small town, but given its size, we were lucky to have a hospital. It covered both North and South Harbor. It's not my first choice for surgery. Larger hospitals in larger communities have more updated equipment. But, in an emergency, it was convenient. Despite the size of the community, the emergency room was surprisingly busy. Judith was taken back to a room first. Nana Jo claimed to be family and was allowed to go with her, while I stayed with Dorothy.

The doctor who examined Dorothy looked about twelve, but he certainly didn't lack confidence. He assured us that he had graduated at the top of his class and was more than competent. No imposter syndrome there. He was positive that Dorothy's ankle was sprained and not broken, but they wheeled her down for X-rays to be sure. I waited for her in the ER. Normally, I can entertain myself watching people, but somehow watching sick or injured people in the emergency room felt invasive.

A wave of sadness washed over me whenever I thought of Nora Cooper. She was obviously in need of help. Would it have made a difference if I had stayed with her at the infirmary? I didn't want to go down that trail of self-doubt. That path was paved with stones labeled *would have, could have, should have*. I knew from experience that the path was dark, and those stones led to a brick wall. I tried, but I couldn't avoid strolling down that dead-end street, at least part of the way. I should be elated. This ordeal was over. Clark Cunningham's death had been a mistake. Obviously, Nora had intended to kill Judith by placing cyanide in her drink, but things had gone wrong when Clark drank the poison instead. Last night, Nora tried again. It was over. Perhaps Nora was finally at peace. Peace? Was that what death was? Peace? I tried to shake the gloomy feeling of darkness that shrouded over me like a blanket. Nora would have called it a negative aura. I smiled. Something bothered me. I forced myself to think, but no matter how hard I tried, the elusive thought just flitted further and further away. I glanced at my watch. I needed to escape. According to the bubbly nurse who drove Dorothy to her X-rays, they were backed up. It would be a couple of hours before she would be done. Physical escape was out of the question. I needed a mental escape. I pulled out my notepad and a pen, and I escaped into the British countryside.

Wickfield Lodge, Servants' Dining Room

Lady Elizabeth could hear the wailing coming from the servants' dining room before she made it to the bottom of the stairs. She braced herself and pushed open the door.

Mrs. Anderson sat at the table with her head buried in her arms. The other servants jumped to attention, but Lady Elizabeth quickly waved her hand, indicating that they were at ease. Lady Elizabeth sat next to the cook and placed a comforting arm around her shoulders.

"Oh, your ladyship," Mrs. Anderson sobbed. "I wish I'd never entered that blasted contest."

"Mrs. Anderson!" Thompkins said.

"It's okay, Thompkins," Lady Elizabeth said. "It's been a harrowing day, and Mrs. Anderson deserves a good cry."

"Begging your ladyship's pardon," Gladys said. "Is it true? Was he really poisoned?"

Mrs. Anderson sobbed louder.

"I'm afraid so," Lady Elizabeth said.

"He ate my cake," Mrs. Anderson said. "Drank some tea. And then keeled over dead. Everyone's going to think it was my cake. They're going to think there was something wrong with my cake."

"There weren't nothing wrong with your cake," Flossie said.

"I ate a piece myself," Jim said. "Look at me. I'm still kicking."

"They'll think I poisoned him, but I swear I never did," Mrs. Anderson said.

Lady Elizabeth patted the cook's back in an attempt to soothe her. "Of course you didn't. We all know that. You didn't have a motive for killing Sebastian Lloyd."

Mrs. Anderson's sobs subsided a bit, and she lifted her head. "They'll think I did it to win that baking contest. Scotland Yard will lock me up and take me to the gallows." She started bawling again.

"But that wouldn't be a reason to kill him," Lady Elizabeth said.

"That's right," Flossie said, taking a seat on the

other side of the cook. "I saw it in a Sherlock Holmes flick with that dishy Basil Rathbone. You have to have a reason . . . a motive for killing someone, or the coppers can't arrest you."

Gladys turned to Lady Elizabeth. "That's right, isn't it?"

"That's right. You need to have a motive—a good motive."

"That rules you out," Jim said. "You've won that baking contest every year for at least a decade. Killing one of the judges certainly wouldn't help you win again. Plus, it was the secretary that got poisoned. Not that idiot colonel."

Mrs. Anderson lifted her head and frowned. "I don't know . . ."

"Well, I do," Frank said. "You didn't need to poison anyone in order to win. You won that contest fair and square. That rules you out. You had no motive."

Thompkins gave a discreet cough. "I do feel that the unseemly display in the drawing room might provide several . . . *suspects* who were angry with both Colonel Livingston and his secretary."

"That's right," Jim said. "Frank and I had to pry them apart last night."

"Why, there were lots of people who wanted that traitor colonel dead," Mrs. McDuffie said. "And I overheard those two MPs arguin' in the rose garden with that secretary just a few hours ago. If anyone had a motive for murder, it was one of them."

Lady Elizabeth turned to the housekeeper. "Mrs. McDuffie, you're brilliant. There were plenty of people with motive. Now, let's put our heads together and figure out which one of them did it."

Chapter 27

"Earth to Sam!" Dorothy Clark waved her hand in front of my face to catch my attention.

"Sorry, I was a million miles away." I put aside my notepad. "Are you done already?"

"Sprained. Not broken, but Doogie Howser wants me to wear this boot." Dorothy lifted her pant leg. "Tylenol for the pain and keep it elevated."

I smiled at the reference to the *Doogie Howser, M.D.* sitcom from the late eighties and early nineties. Dorothy's doctor had looked young, but he wasn't a teenage genius who earned a perfect score on his SATs at age six, graduated from Princeton at age ten, and completed medical school by age fourteen. Still, I smiled while I walked to the car and drove to pick up Dorothy at the door.

Nana Jo responded to my text by saying she planned to stay at the hospital with Judith a little longer, and that I should take Dorothy home and then go home and get some sleep. I wasn't sure why she wanted to stay. Surely, Judith Hunter was no longer in any danger. Nora Cooper murdered Clark Cunningham, and now Nora Cooper was dead, too. It didn't make any sense, but I was tired and my brain wasn't firing on all cylinders. I needed to rest. I told Nana Jo to text me later when she was ready to go home.

I dropped Dorothy off at Shady Acres Retirement Village. Then I drove home. I was exhausted, and the idea of a long, hot shower and then crawling in between the sheets of my bed sounded like the best plan I'd ever heard.

The shower was glorious. However, once I got in bed, sleep eluded me. I don't know if it was the fact that it was now broad daylight and my internal clock was thrown off, the bright sunlight that streamed in through the blinds, or the noise of movement and people in the bookstore that kept me awake. Whatever the reason, I tossed and turned but I did not sleep. My mind played and replayed what I knew of Nora Cooper.

Nora Cooper was unhinged. She accused Judith Hunter of stealing her book, even though Judith claimed she'd bought the manuscript. Nora Cooper blamed Judith for stealing her boyfriend. That much was true. Although, I was reluctant to place all of the blame for that on Judith. By all accounts, Clark Cunningham was a willing participant. Judith didn't force herself on him. He made a choice. Just as Paul West made a choice to cheat on his wife. At least Nora and Clark Cunningham weren't married. My views on marriage were old-fashioned. I believed a vow was a vow. It didn't sound like Olivia and Paul had an open marriage. Olivia would have mentioned it. Wouldn't she? Open marriage . . . what a concept. Times had changed a lot since Leon and I were married. Now, here I was planning for another wedding. What if Frank wanted an open marriage? What if he got bored with me? Would I have behaved differently than Olivia Townsend? Would I have gotten plastic surgery to make myself more appealing? I glanced at Snickers, who was curled up in a ball and snoring less than a foot from my face.

"No. If Frank cheated on me with another woman, I'd probably take Nana Jo's Peacemaker and shoot him."

At the sound of my voice, Snickers opened one eye.

I reached out a hand to pet her and she rolled over onto her back, exposing her stomach. I complied and scratched her belly.

She relaxed and closed her eyes, using her paw to guide my hand to the appropriate place.

I absentmindedly scratched.

"I may be old-fashioned, but I'm not totally naïve. People change. Relationships change. But I don't think women have changed that much. Olivia Townsend might have tried to kill her rival."

What about Scarlet MacDunkin? Scarlet was one bitter woman. She hated Judith Hunter. She admitted that she wanted Judith dead. "What am I doing? Nora was the killer. Case closed." I sat up.

"This is ridiculous. I need a distraction." I climbed out of bed.

Snickers stared at me. She watched me go over to my desk and turn on my laptop.

Oreo stretched.

"Maybe if I write, I'll be able to close the door on this murder once and for all."

Snickers stood up on the bed and turned around in circles. After the third circle, she lay back down and went back to sleep.

Wickfield Lodge, Drawing Room

Lord William Marsh sat in a chair with his foot propped up on a footstool. The family's Cavalier King

Charles spaniel, Cuddles, was curled up on the floor next to the chair.

Lady Elizabeth sat on the sofa, with her knitting next to her. Lady Penelope paced from the chair where her husband, Lord Victor, sat smoking to the fireplace where her brother-in-law, Lord James Browning, smoked.

Thompkins entered, coughed discreetly, and then announced, "Detective Inspector Covington."

The Scotland Yard detective was tall, lean, and gangly with thick curly hair. He was well-known to the Marsh family and was now engaged to marry their cousin, Lady Clara Trewellen-Harper.

The Scotland Yard detective greeted the members of the family.

"Peter, I was hoping you'd get assigned to this case," Lady Elizabeth said.

"I'm rather surprised. I didn't think the chief was very keen on sending me, but I suspected he got a nudge." Detective Inspector Covington glanced at Lord Browning.

"I'll admit Budgy wasn't exactly thrilled at the idea. He thought Peter might be too close to the case, but once I assured him that the family's only connection was allowing the village to host the fete on their property, and were completely clear on this one, he didn't object too much." James shrugged.

Chief Inspector Albert Buddington happened to be Lord Browning's godfather, to whom he had been known as "Budgy" the majority of the duke's life.

"Is Clara coming down?" Lady Penelope asked.

"Not this time. She's neck deep in top secret work at Bletchley Park, or a stampede of wild antelope wouldn't have been able to keep her away. She is planning to come to Kingfordshire to see Daphne and hopefully, the new Lord Browning." The detective grinned.

"How is she?" Lady Elizabeth asked.

"Wonderful. She loves the work she's doing, although she can't talk about it. Although, she's driving me insane picking out silver, china, and towels. I had no idea there were so many decisions to make when planning a wedding." The detective glanced at his two soon-to-be cousins, who both nodded.

"Wait until you have to choose baby names." Lord Browning rubbed the back of his neck.

"Well, send her our love," Lady Elizabeth said.

There was a tentative knock on the door and then Mrs. McDuffie pushed the door open and stuck her head inside.

"Please come in, Mrs. McDuffie," Lady Elizabeth said.

Mrs. McDuffie was followed by Jim, Frank, Gladys, and Flossie. There was a whispered conversation and then a red-faced Mrs. Anderson reluctantly entered, followed by Thompkins.

"Won't you please be seated?" Lady Elizabeth said.

Thompkins stepped forward. "If your ladyship doesn't mind, we would prefer to stand."

The staff nodded.

Lady Elizabeth nodded. "Whatever makes you the most comfortable."

"Okay, what's going on?" Detective Inspector Covington asked.

"I think we can save a great deal of time by working more closely together on this case. So, I asked the staff if they would join us and share what they've seen." Lady Elizabeth pulled out her knitting and turned to the staff. "Who would like to go first?"

"Beggin' your ladyship's pardon. I'll start." Mrs. McDuffie stepped forward.

"Wonderful." Lady Elizabeth nodded.

"I was taking the wash off the lines when I 'eard them two MPs arguing out in the rose garden with that secretary."

"What did you hear?" Detective Inspector Covington asked.

"I weren't listenin', you understand."

"Of course not. The thought never crossed my mind," D.I. Covington said.

Satisfied, the housekeeper continued. "Well, like I said, I was taking down the wash. That's when I 'eard loud voices. Those two MPs, Birdwhistle and Bythesea, said, 'Listen 'ere, you double-dealing nitwit, either you put an end to that book or we will.' That's when Lloyd laughed. 'I thought England was a free nation,' he said. Well, that just got my blood boiling. I don't take kindly to nobody putting down England."

"Especially not some furiner," Gladys mumbled.

"What was that?" Lady Elizabeth turned to Gladys.

Poor Gladys's face got as red as a beet. "I'm sorry. I didn't mean to interrupt."

"Not at all. We're all here to get to the truth." She smiled encouragingly. "How did you know that Sebastian Lloyd was foreign?"

Gladys gave a tentative glance at the housekeeper, who nodded for her to continue. "I heard him talking in another language."

"Did you recognize what language it was?" Lord Browning asked.

The maid shook her head. "I don't know no other language but my own," she said.

"Do you think you would recognize it if you heard it again?" Lord Browning asked.

Gladys frowned. "I don't know . . ."

"Let's try. Did it sound like this? *C'est une belle journée pour une promenade dans la campagne.*" Lord Browning watched the maid for a glimmer of recognition.

Gladys thought but then shook her head. "That sounds pretty, but it weren't like that. It was more . . . rough."

"How about this, *Es ist ein schöner Tag für einen Spaziergang auf dem Land.*"

"That's it. It sounded like that," Gladys said.

Lady Elizabeth and Lord Browning exchanged a glance.

Jim and Frank repeated what they'd heard the previous night as they were hauling the battling MPs out.

"Fantastic. You've all been very helpful," Lady Elizabeth said.

The staff nodded and then turned and left.

"Thompkins, I'd like you to stay," Lady Elizabeth said.

The butler held the door for the others and then closed it and returned to his stiff position on the wall.

D.I. Covington glanced from Lady Elizabeth to Lord Browning. "Maybe someone can fill me in on what brought two British MPs, a retired colonel, and what I believe must be a German private secretary to blows in the home of the king's cousin?"

"Good Lord, when you say it like that it sounds like a bad joke," Victor said.

"Trust me. I'm not joking," the detective said.

Lady Elizabeth briefly explained what led to the dinner party and book reading moving at the last minute from Lady Dallyripple's home to Wickfield Lodge.

When she finished, the detective turned to Lord Browning. "Anything you want to tell me about why MI5 is involved?"

"Officially, MI5 is *not* involved. I'm merely here visiting family," Lord Browning said.

"Okay, how about unofficially?"

Lord Browning gave a brief explanation about the concerns around Colonel Livingston's new book and what he might possibly disclose.

D.I. Covington stared at the duke. "I don't suppose you . . . never mind." He shook his head.

Lord Browning raised his brows. "MI5 doesn't assassinate our fellow citizens."

"Sorry, I didn't mean to insult—"

Lord Browning waved away his protest. "No worries, ol' boy." He grinned. "Perhaps, if it were Colonel Bloody Livingston, instead of the lowly secretary who bit the bullet, you might be justified in thinking that His Majesty's government might intervene."

Lady Elizabeth had been sitting quietly, but she stopped and put down her knitting needles and stared into space. "That's it."

"What's it?" D.I. Covington said.

"There's nothing wrong with the cake. The judges ate Mrs. Anderson's cake and they're all fine. After the competition, they sliced up the cake into small pieces and lots of people ate it. The poison had to be in the tea." Lady Elizabeth looked at her family around the room.

"We haven't tested the teacup yet, but okay, I'll bite. What difference does that make?" D.I. Covington asked.

"But don't you see? Sebastian Lloyd dropped his teacup and Colonel Livingston gave him his cup. That poison wasn't intended for Sebastian Lloyd. It was meant for Colonel Livingston. Livingston was the intended victim."

Chapter 28

My peaceful excursion into the British countryside was disturbed when Oreo suddenly bounded out of the room barking. Snickers was a few seconds behind, but quickly leapt from the bed. It took me a few moments to reorient myself. When I didn't immediately follow, Snickers rushed to my bedroom doorway and barked as if to say, *Are you coming?*

"What's going on?" I asked, as though I expected an answer.

Snickers cocked her head to the side and stared. Then, she hurried after her brother.

It was broad daylight and close to ten in the morning; chances of a burglary were slim, so I left my trusty Louisville Slugger in the closet and walked to the living room. Only then did I hear the commotion below.

Loud voices and the rumble of feet propelled me downstairs.

It took a bit of maneuvering to get the door open without letting the poodles escape, but I managed it. Once downstairs, the noise was much louder. I turned the corner and rushed into the bookstore to find the store jam-packed with people.

From my tiptoes, I caught sight of Nana Jo's head and I elbowed my way through the crowds toward her. Once I was at the front of the store, I was finally able to see what caused the commotion. Judith Hunter was surrounded by reporters with television cameras and microphones pointed at her as she was being interviewed.

What the . . . ? I mouthed to my grandmother.

"She insisted on coming for her book signing. The doctors wanted to keep her overnight, but . . ." She shrugged.

"But where did all of these people come from?"

"Beats me. I was tempted to fire my Peacemaker and throw them all out, but Judith said the publicity would be good for business." Nana Jo shrugged.

I waved my hands over my head in an attempt to get everyone's attention, but it was fruitless.

Nana Jo put her fingers to her mouth and let out a loud whistle as though she were hailing a taxi in New York City.

The rumble died down and everyone turned to face me.

"I want to thank everyone for coming out today, but we are going to need to have those buying books to form a line starting here and going outside."

There was a rumble of dissent from the crowd.

"I'm sorry, but it's a fire hazard to have this many people in the store at one time. I'd like to ask the press to please wait in the conference room or outside until after the book signing."

There was a roar of dissent from the reporters, which Nana Jo squashed. "Your cameras are taking space away from paying customers and Ms. Hunter's fans."

The crowd applauded and the reporters must have realized they were vastly outnumbered.

Judith raised her hands and plastered on a smile. "Mrs. Washington's right. I'll be happy to sign all of your books and answer whatever questions the press has for me, but we must be respectful."

The crowd applauded.

The next few minutes were filled with shuffling as people formed a long line that wrapped around the store and then flowed outside while the media hauled their lights, cameras, and other equipment into the conference room where I held meetings.

Judith made her way to the counter. "I'm terribly sorry. I didn't mean to cause such a disruption." She gave me a sheepish grin.

"How did the press find out you were here?" I asked.

"I posted on my social media account that I was going to be here today. I guess my publicist must have taken it and sent it to all of the news agencies in the area." Judith stopped to acknowledge a fan and take a photo.

Nana Jo whispered, "She sure moves fast. I thought Clark Cunningham was her publicist."

"So did I." I glanced around the store. "She's right about one thing. The publicity is bound to be good for business."

"We'd better get busy. You can't have gotten much sleep. Are you sure you're up to this?" Nana Jo asked.

"You've probably had less sleep than me."

"Yeah, but I'm old. I don't need as much sleep as you do." Nana Jo smiled.

Between the two of us, we were able to keep the crowds under control and manage the chaos. The constant stream of customers kept us busy. After an hour, Nana Jo announced that we were out of copies of Judith's book. There was a rumble that threatened to erupt, but Nana Jo headed it off. She held up a box of labels. "We do have bookplates, and if you order a copy of the book, we will give you a bookplate that Judith can sign. That way, when your book arrives, you'll be able to add the signature."

That soothed the crowd and I placed orders for fifty books. The bookplates that Nana Jo was using were mine, so while I was placing the book orders, I ordered a couple extra boxes. Honestly, it was a great idea. I could get authors to sign a sheet or two of labels and add them to books.

Eventually, the last person left with their receipt for their copy of *The Corpse Danced at Midnight*, along with their signed bookplate. I stretched and glanced at the time. The two-hour book signing had lasted over three hours. Judith then spent an hour answering questions from reporters. It was nearly two in the afternoon. My stomach growled to let me know that I hadn't eaten yet.

"I'm starving," I announced to Nana Jo.

"Then I arrived just in time."

I turned to see Scarlet MacDunkin with a broad smile on her face. With a bit of effort, I converted my *What on earth are you doing here?* surprised look into a *What a pleasant surprise!* surprised look. I must not have been successful because Scarlet chuckled.

"Surprised to see me?"

I glanced over to the side where Judith was finishing her interviews with the media. She glanced at us from the corner of her eye and scowled.

Scarlet blew her a kiss and then threw her head back and cackled. "Oh my word. The look of hatred on her face is worth every dime I spent getting here."

"Other than tormenting Judith, why are you here?" I asked.

"Would you believe that I've been craving corn chowder and a BLT served by that deliciously attractive fiancé of yours?" She paused, but then quickly got serious. "Actually, that part's true. Today's my last day in town and I was determined to try and get another serving of that creamy deliciousness before I go home. On my drive here, imagine my surprise at hearing on the radio that poor Judith had recovered from her near-death experience with Nora and was well enough to not only sign books at Market Street Mysteries, but was giving interviews to the press."

"This book signing was arranged ahead of time. You're making it sound as though she just decided to do it after . . . after last night." I shivered.

Scarlet tilted her head to the side. "You really are naïve, aren't you?"

Nana Jo folded her arms across her chest. "Frank's restaurant is down the street. What's your aim in coming here, other than insulting my granddaughter?"

"*Grrr*. I poked the grandmama bear," Scarlet said.

"You sure did indeed. Only, this grandmama bear isn't like those sappy bears that allowed Goldilocks to trespass in their home, eat their food, break their furniture, and sleep in their beds. This grandmama bear will rip your hair out by its mousy brown roots and bend you like a pretzel for coming into this bookstore and insulting my granddaughter." Nana Jo glared.

Scarlet's smile slid off her face. She stared at Nana Jo for several seconds.

Nana Jo didn't blink.

"You're right. I'm sorry," Scarlet said, and for the first time since I met her, I truly believed she was sincere. "Samantha has been nothing but kind to me. The book signing yesterday was amazing and she deserves to be treated with respect." She turned and looked me in the eyes. "Please, accept my apology."

"Thank you," I said.

"Now, why are you really here?" Nana Jo asked.

"I really did come for food. Plus, I heard about Nora and I thought maybe I'd horn in on some of Judith's publicity."

The door to the conference room opened and one of the cameramen walked out.

Nana Jo hailed another taxi with her whistle. "Hey, look who showed up. Mystery author, Scarlet MacDunkin."

The reporters looked puzzled, but didn't seem to bite the bait Nana Jo was dangling in front of them.

Nana Jo turned to Scarlet. "You were close friends with Nora Cooper, weren't you?"

That caught their attention. Within seconds it was Lights. Camera. Action. Microphones were thrust in front of Scarlet and she was now the center of attention.

Nana Jo and I stepped back so we were out of line of sight of the cameras.

Judith Hunter fumed, with her arms folded across her chest.

"My work here is done. Now, I'm going to pick up lunch for four from Frank's." Nana Jo grabbed her purse and headed out.

Chapter 29

It turns out Nana Jo only needed lunch for three. Judith Hunter claimed that she had another panel and had to leave. I offered to drive, but she'd had one of the students bring her car to the hospital last night, or rather this morning. So she left before Nana Jo returned.

My assistant, Dawson Alexander, came home from football practice and took over managing the store, which was a lot less hectic now that Judith Hunter was gone, while Scarlet, Nana Jo, and I ate lunch.

Frank's corn chowder was as heavenly as ever and my BLT was perfect. We ate in silence for several minutes. When we were all satisfyingly full, Nana Jo broke the silence.

"What really brought you down here?"

"I told you. I—"

"Horse pucky!" Nana Jo said. "Now, spill it. And skip the love affair with Frank's corn chowder. We'll concede that."

Scarlet picked at the remains of her sandwich while Nana Jo and I waited. Most people couldn't stand silence. They felt compelled to fill it with something. Scarlet MacDunkin was no different.

"I've already admitted wanting to horn in on Judith's publicity." She sighed. "I've been angry with Judith so long, that I couldn't resist one last opportunity to poke her."

"Poke her how?" I asked.

She shrugged. "I don't know, but something about this whole thing stinks to high heaven. Nora was making a fuss about Judith stealing her book. She said she had proof." She turned to me. "You remember, that day you were hiding in the closet eavesdropping, you heard her, too."

"I was not hiding. I was . . . oh, never mind. Yes, I remember Nora saying she had proof. So what?"

"Well, what if she did?" Scarlet looked from me to Nana Jo.

"Then, she could have sued Judith and maybe made a lot of money," Nana Jo said.

Scarlet wiped her hands on a napkin and leaned forward. "Listen, I know it may not seem like it, but I actually liked Nora."

"That sounds a lot like the old proverb, 'The enemy of my enemy is my friend,'" I said.

Scarlet smiled. "Okay, granted. Our mutual hatred of Judith Hunter was one thing that bound Nora and I together. But, let's face the truth. You met Nora. Would you ever in a million years think hippy-dippy-I-see-dead-people-Nora-Cooper was capable of pulling off a murder in front of a room full of people?"

I thought back on the few interactions I had with Nora. "I'll admit Nora didn't seem . . . artful enough for a stunt like that, but when someone is bent on revenge, there's no telling what they might do."

"Like me?" Scarlet asked.

I didn't need a mirror to know that a flush had risen up my neck.

"I didn't know Nora Cooper, but based on what Sam has told me, it sounds like her elevator wasn't making it all the way to the top floor. Maybe she snapped completely. What do you think, Sam?"

"Nora wasn't stable, but I didn't think she was dangerous, but I'm not an expert on mental illness," I said.

"She wasn't dangerous," Scarlet argued.

"I was there. I saw Nora Cooper trying to push Judith Hunter off that cliff," Nana Jo said.

"Are you sure that's what you saw?" Scarlet asked.

"I may be old, but I'm not senile. If that's what you're getting at."

"I didn't mean to imply that you were. All I'm asking is are you sure that Nora was the one trying to push Judith off the bluffs? Could it have been the other way around?"

Nana Jo paused. "You mean, could it have been Judith trying to push Nora off the cliff?"

"Sometimes, when two people are struggling, it's hard to tell who's the aggressor and who's merely trying to protect themselves." Scarlet stared at Nana Jo.

Chapter 30

"That's an interesting theory, but do you have any evidence to back it up?" Nana Jo asked.

Scarlet shook her head.

"Okay, you're obsessed with Judith Hunter and allowing your hatred to cloud your reason. Let's take a step back. Who else might have a reason to want Judith dead?" Nana Jo asked.

"Other than me?" Scarlet chuckled. "My money would be on Olivia Townsend."

"Why Olivia?" I asked.

"Because she's not as dumb as she looks."

"Meaning?" I already knew the answer, but I wondered how much Scarlet knew.

"Meaning, that Olivia has to know that Paul and Judith are still having an affair."

I exchanged a glance with Nana Jo. "What do you mean? Olivia told me just yesterday that the affair was over."

Scarlet snorted. "Olivia has joined the cult that believes if you say something often enough, that makes it true."

"How do you know the affair isn't over?" Nana Jo asked.

"I'll admit, I have been obsessed with Judith Hunter. I attend the same events. Sometimes I'm able to get on panels. Sometimes I just sit in the audience, surrounded by her fans." She rolled her eyes and paused. "Sometimes, I may sit outside her house and wait for her to leave so I can follow her." She took a deep breath.

"And while you were stalking her, you saw . . ." I prompted.

"I saw her and Paul sneaking out together. They've been at several of the same events and they always manage to stay at the same hotels."

"But they both write mysteries. It's not uncommon that they would be at the same conferences. There aren't that many of them," I said.

"A few months ago, Paul and Judith were both at the In Your Write Mind Writers Workshop in Greensburg, Pennsylvania. Judith was the guest speaker for a local university's writing program on the same campus. The mystery writers always have a Murder Mystery Dinner at an Italian restaurant. One of the professors, Victoria Thompson, writes a mystery—"

"Victoria Thompson? The author of the Gaslight Mystery series?" I asked.

Scarlet nodded.

"I love her books. I wonder if—"

"Sam, you're getting off track. Focus." Nana Jo brought me back to reality.

"Sorry. Please continue."

"Where was I? Oh yeah, so we're all at the restaurant and I noticed that Paul was sitting across from Judith. She was, of course, playing the lead role." Scarlet rolled her eyes. "Anyway, he got this strange look on his face. So, I dropped my napkin deliberately on purpose, and under the table, Judith was rubbing her foot up his leg. I nearly gagged."

"Was Olivia there?" Nana Jo asked.

"Yep." Scarlet nodded.

Nana Jo and I exchanged a look.

"Did Olivia drop her napkin, too?" I asked.

"Her purse, actually." Scarlet grinned.

"I don't suppose her purse had some help making its way to the floor, did it?" Nana Jo asked.

Scarlet opened her mouth in wide-eyed shock. "Would I do something like that?"

"In a New York minute," Nana Jo said.

"I plead the Fifth. The important thing isn't who might have *helped* her see what was going on under the table. The critical thing here is did she know that Paul and Judith are still playing footsie. I say she knows."

"Olivia might have a reason to want Judith dead, but what would be her motivation for killing Nora?" I asked.

"Beats me. My money is still on Judith," Scarlet said.

We tossed around a few other ideas, but nothing stuck.

After Scarlet left, Nana Jo and I sat at the bistro table at the back of the bookshop and rehashed everything we knew about Judith Hunter, Clark Cunningham, and Nora Cooper. Which, in the grand scheme of things, didn't amount to much.

Nana Jo wasn't as engaged in the conversation as she normally was and after a few minutes, she drifted off into her own world.

I waved my hand in front of her face. "Nana Jo."

"Sorry, I was . . . somewhere else."

"Reliving the fight on the bluffs?" I guessed.

Nana Jo nodded. "Scarlet has a good point. We weren't there from the beginning, so we didn't see how the fight started. By the time Dorothy and I got there, they were locked together and grappling to get the other one over the edge. I got distracted for a second when I thought I saw someone else nearby, but it was dark and Judith needed help."

"It could have been the way Scarlet said."

Nana Jo nodded.

"But why?"

"I mean, Nora Cooper certainly had a good reason to hate Judith Hunter. She'd stolen her boyfriend, Clark Cunningham. She tricked her into selling her manuscript, which later went on to become a huge success." Nana Jo shook her head. "I think that would be enough to make me want to wring her neck."

"But, you're a lot stronger than Nora Cooper. You would have horsewhipped Judith Hunter. Trussed her up like a Thanksgiving turkey and dragged her into court."

Nana Jo smiled. "True."

Suddenly, a light bulb went on. "That's just it. Nora Cooper didn't just want money. She wanted *everyone* to know that she'd written that book."

Nana Jo stared. "Okay."

"Don't you see? She needed Judith Hunter alive for that. If Judith were dead, she wouldn't be able to humiliate her in court. She wouldn't have the pleasure of seeing Judith squirm when the judge ruled in her favor. Or see Judith with egg on her face have to admit that she didn't actually write the manuscript."

"So, you think Judith Hunter lured Nora to the bluffs with the intent of tossing her over the side into Lake Michigan?"

"Maybe . . . I don't know. I mean, it seems sketchy. Judith was really confident that she legally owned the manuscript. If it did make it to court, she might be embarrassed, but I don't know if Nora would have won."

"Where do we go from here? As far as Stinky Pitt is concerned, this thing is all wrapped up. Nora put the poison in Judith's glass, but Clark Cunningham drank it accidentally.

Nora made another attempt to kill Judith last night, but lost her footing and ended up killing herself," Nana Jo said.

"If Nora Cooper wasn't the killer, that means the real killer is still out there. And Judith Hunter could still be in danger."

"Then, we better get back to work." Nana Jo rose from her chair.

Chapter 31

I was done with all of my panels for the book festival until Sunday morning, but since Judith Hunter wasn't done, Nana Jo and I went back to keep an eye on her. Just in case.

I didn't think Judith's panels could have been more crowded than the one yesterday, but I was wrong.

Just as Judith Hunter came onto the stage, the room erupted in applause.

Nana Jo was taller than me and able to see over the crowds. "Looks like the fire marshal is about to shut this down."

"Why? What's happening?" I struggled to see, but even on the tips of my toes, it was useless.

"Fire marshal's talking to Dr. Leonard Peters and a short woman I suspect is Mrs. Graves."

After a few moments, Mrs. Graves walked onto the stage and motioned for the crowd to be quiet. She took the microphone that was on stage for the moderator.

"I have just been informed by the fire marshal that we will not be able to continue the panel discussion with Judith

Hunter today, because we are in violation of the fire safety regulations."

The crowd booed.

"She better be careful. She could end up with a riot," Nana Jo said.

Some of the people in the back started stomping their feet and chanting. "Hell No, We Won't Go!"

Mrs. Graves tried to speak, but the crowd simply chanted, stomped, and clapped louder. Eventually, Judith Hunter took her microphone.

"I believe Mrs. Graves has an alternative. Please be respectful and give her your attention."

The crowd settled down.

Mrs. Graves thanked Judith. "As I was about to say, we are going to move this panel outside to the north quad. We are setting up now, so if you'll all make your way outside, we should be able to accommodate everyone who would like to hear Miss Hunter."

The crowd cheered. A wave of people got up and made their way toward the door. Nana Jo and I were carried along with the swell. For once, I was grateful to be at the back of the room. That meant we were among the first outside.

Freed from the confines of the auditorium, Nana Jo and I moved away from the horde. We stepped into the hallway rather than heading toward the door and allowed the wave to pass around us.

It didn't take long for the crowd surge to dwindle down to a trickle. Like lemmings, the crowd headed outside. We were about to follow when we caught a glimpse of Olivia Townsend and Paul West following the other lemmings.

"I'm trailing Judith. Let me guess, you two are trailing Paul and Barbie."

We turned and saw Dorothy Clark standing behind us.

"Why aren't you at home resting?" Nana Jo asked.

"Because I'm fully capable of doing my job. Thank you very much."

"Honestly, Dorothy. You need to take care of yourself. Wait, why are you here? With Nora Cooper dead, the case is over," I said.

"When I got home, I started thinking. What if Nora Cooper wasn't the killer? I mean, when I saw her, she didn't strike me as the type who'd go for physical violence. She wasn't very big. Judith Hunter is physically fit. No way Nora could have taken her. So, I thought maybe I need to keep watching. Just in case. Besides, I still have an article to write." Dorothy held up a notepad. "Now, your turn. Why are you two here?"

"Same reason," Nana Jo said.

I told Dorothy about the book signing and the visit from Scarlet MacDunkin.

"Well, there's certainly no point in all of us trailing one woman. I'm following through on my assignment. You two are welcome to stay, or perhaps you'd like to update Stinky Pitt over there. He looks like a lost lamb."

I glanced around and saw Detective Pitt standing in a corner. When he caught us looking in his direction, he stopped holding up the wall and joined our group.

"Detective Pitt, I'm surprised to see you. What brings you out today? I would have thought you'd be tying a bow around your file and celebrating," Nana Jo said.

"Just wrapping up a few loose ends." He rolled back and forth on the balls of his feet.

Nana Jo narrowed her gaze. "Oh, like what?"

Detective Pitt frowned. I could almost see the wheels turning in his head. Did he share with us? Or did he keep his cards close to his chest? I decided to help him out.

"You're not one hundred percent certain that Nora Cooper murdered Clark Cunningham either, are you?"

"What do you mean, either? All of the evidence points to Nora Cooper." He dodged answering the question.

"Dorothy, it looks like you'd better keep an eye on Judith Hunter, but no heroics this time. Call for backup if anything exciting happens," Nana Jo ordered.

Dorothy saluted and limped outside.

"Perhaps we should take this conversation someplace a little more private," I suggested.

We headed to the green room behind the stage. With Judith Hunter's panel moved outside, it was empty.

Nana Jo opened the closet door and verified it was empty before sitting down.

I could feel the flush in my cheeks at the memory of being discovered the first time I'd met Judith Hunter, but sat on the sofa and waited patiently.

Nana Jo and I stared at Detective Pitt. Experience told us he wouldn't be able to withstand both the stares and the silence and we were proven right.

"Alright, no need to give me the death stare." Detective Pitt glared. "Yesterday when Nora Cooper was in this room, she was a basket case. I could see her poisoning Judith Hunter, but I just didn't think she was the type to get physical. That's all."

I wasn't sure if I should be impressed that Detective Pitt came to the same conclusion that I had regarding Nora's mental state. Or, if I should be worried. He wasn't, as Nana Jo said, the sharpest knife in the drawer. "We came to the same conclusion."

"You did?" He looked surprised.

"Nora wasn't mentally, physically, or emotionally strong. Maybe if she had a weapon, she could have threatened Judith."

"Did she have a weapon?" Nana Jo asked.

"According to Judith Hunter, she pointed a gun, but we never recovered it," Detective Pitt said. "But that doesn't mean anything. It could have gotten flung from her hand by the impact of hitting the rocks."

"If it got washed out into the Lake Michigan surge, it could be halfway to the Gulf of Mexico by now," Nana Jo said.

"Exactly," Detective Pitt agreed.

"But she was there. She was wrestling with Judith Hunter in the middle of the night. That much is true. You saw her." I turned to Nana Jo.

"We did see her. We saw the two women wrestling and we saw Nora tumbling over the bluffs," Nana Jo said.

"Do we know for a fact that Nora called Judith?" I asked.

Detective Pitt shook his head. "We're checking Nora Cooper's cell phone records. The good news is we don't need a warrant when the person is dead. Otherwise, it could take weeks to get through the legal red tape."

"Any calls to Judith Hunter?" I asked.

"That's the problem. So far, we haven't been able to confirm that Nora Cooper called Judith Hunter." Detective Pitt took a pen and used it to scratch his back.

"I don't suppose there's a way to prove if Judith Hunter called Nora?" I asked.

Detective Pitt grinned. "We would need a warrant to check Judith Hunter's cell phone records, but . . ."

"But since you don't need a warrant to check Nora Cooper's cell, you can determine if she received a call from Judith Hunter," Nana Jo said.

"Exactly." Detective Pitt beamed.

"Well? What did you find?" Nana Jo asked.

The smile fell from Pitt's face. "So far nothing, but that's not to say that Judith Hunter didn't use another phone. She might have used the phone from her hotel room or maybe she had a burner phone. We do know that Nora Cooper received a call around the time in question, but we can't track the phone. Not yet anyway."

"Where do we go from here?" Nana Jo asked.

Both Detective Pitt and Nana Jo turned and looked at me.

"We keep an eye on Judith Hunter. If she's the murderer, then we'll need to keep searching for evidence to prove it," I said.

"And if she isn't?" Nana Jo asked.

"If she isn't, then we have to assume the murderer is going to try again, and we'll need to be ready."

Chapter 32

Detective Pitt went back to the station and Nana Jo went to help Dorothy keep an eye on Judith Hunter.

Alone in the green room, I rehashed everything in my mind. Could Judith Hunter be the killer? If so, that would mean that Judith deliberately poisoned her own glass, knowing that she wouldn't drink it. It would also mean that Judith Hunter lured Nora Cooper to the bluffs and deliberately shoved her over the side to her death. Again, why? My brain felt like I'd just spent a few rounds on a carousel. I took out my notebook and pen. Nana Jo always said writing helped my subconscious figure out whodunit. With less than twenty-four hours left before the book festival was over and everyone went about their own way, I needed to figure things out quickly.

Wickfield Lodge, Drawing Room

Colonel Basil Livingston stormed into the drawing room. "Those Neanderthals posing as policemen told me that I'd find the person in charge in here." He glanced around.

D.I. Covington stood and extended a hand. "I'm Detective Inspector Covington with Scotland Yard. How may I help you?"

Colonel Livingston ignored the hand. "I demand to know what is being done to find the deranged person who murdered my secretary."

Before Detective Inspector Covington could respond, the two MPs pushed through the doors and entered the study.

"This is insufferable," Major Birdwhistle said.

"For once, I agree," Sir Greyson Bythesea said.

Lord William pounded his fist on the arm of his chair. "How dare you just barge in without so much as a by-your-leave. This is my home, not some public house."

Major Birdwhistle's cheeks flushed. Whether from genuine regret for his unseemly behavior or a desire to stay on the good side of a member of the House of Lords and someone with connections to His Majesty, wasn't clear. Regardless, he mumbled an apology.

"Terribly sorry, ol' man," Sir Greyson said.

"Gentlemen, this entire ordeal must be extremely stressful for all of you. Won't you all please sit down." Lady Elizabeth turned to her nephew. "Victor, per-

haps you could ask Thompkins to bring tea, or perhaps something stronger?"

Colonel Livingston glared at the MPs. He took out
a handkerchief and wiped his forehead. "Why, yes.
You're right. It has been extremely trying. Perhaps a
whiskey and soda would help to steady my nerves."

The MPs both nodded their agreement to whis-
keys.

Lady Elizabeth nodded to Victor, who rose and
went to see to the drinks.

Bythesea and Birdwhistle found seats as far away
from Colonel Livingston as it was possible to be while
remaining in the same room.

"Now, gentlemen, this is Detective Inspector
Peter Covington. He's one of the finest detectives
Scotland Yard has and even recently assisted His
Majesty with a matter of national security. So, you
can certainly rely on his discretion," Lady Elizabeth
said.

Colonel Livingston gazed at the detective with a
bit more respect than he'd shown previously. "Well . . .
of course . . . certainly. Pleased to meet you." He
rose and extended his hand. His ears flushed red,
perhaps from remembering his earlier snub.

D.I. Covington gracefully shook Livingston's hand
and then followed up by shaking the two MPs' hands
as each was introduced.

By the time the introductions were over, Thompkins returned. He pushed a cart with a bottle of
whiskey, soda, and a tray laden with tea. He filled the
whiskey glasses and spritzed each with soda, then
distributed them to the men.

Lady Elizabeth poured tea for Lady Penelope,
Lord William, and herself.

Lord William scowled at the tea, but sipped it in silence.

"Now, Colonel Livingston, I believe you had something you wanted to say." Lady Elizabeth sipped her tea.

"Well . . . I was . . . concerned that the murderer would get away in the crowd while the police were focused on interrogating me." Colonel Livingston tossed back his drink and then stared at his empty glass.

"Would you care for another?" Victor asked. Gaining a grateful nod from the colonel, he took the glass and refilled it.

"Thank you." Colonel Livingston accepted the glass. This time he sipped the amber liquid.

"Colonel Livingston, do you know anyone who would want to kill your secretary?" D.I. Covington asked.

"Me? Of course not. Why would anyone want to kill Sebastian? He was an excellent secretary," Colonel Livingston said.

"I'm sure he was. Although, I do believe that several members of the Marsh staff overheard Sebastian Lloyd arguing with several people over the past twenty-four hours. Including yourself, Major Birdwhistle, and Sir Greyson." D.I. Covington flipped back in his notebook as though verifying his facts and then turned his attention to each of the men.

Sir Greyson Bythesea cleared his throat. "I want to apologize for my conduct last night. It was inexcusable. I'm embarrassed and ashamed and I beg your forgiveness."

"I too want to apologize. I allowed my emotions to get the better of me. Please accept my sincere apology." Major Birdwhistle stood and bowed to both Lady Elizabeth and Lord William.

Colonel Livingston coughed. "Well . . . I too feel that an apology is due to your lord and ladyship."

Lady Penelope's lips twitched at the colonel's mention of an apology without actually offering one. However, she quickly hid it by taking a sip of her tea.

"Thank you, all," Lady Elizabeth said.

D.I. Covington tried again. "Now that you've gotten that out, perhaps we can focus on *who* wanted to kill Sebastian Lloyd."

"I'm sure I have no idea. Sebastian Lloyd was merely a member of my staff, not a family member. He didn't take me into his confidences, and I have no idea what he did outside of handling my correspondence." Colonel Livingston leaned back in his seat with a pleased look on his face.

"Major Birdwhistle? You and Sir Greyson were overheard in a heated argument with Lloyd. Would you mind telling me what the argument was about?" D.I. Covington asked.

The two MPs exchanged a look. Eventually, an agreement was made. Major Birdwhistle tugged at his collar, and then cleared his throat. "We were both concerned about Colonel Livingston's book and his traitorous intention of sharing British military secrets with the enemy. It seemed to us that he was—"

"How dare you!" Colonel Livingston bounced up.

D.I. Covington immediately stepped in between the two men. "Sit down, or I'll have both of you locked up for disorderly conduct."

Livingston scowled, but returned to his seat.

"Now, I believe you were explaining why you

were arguing with the deceased," D.I. Covington reminded the MP.

"I was simply explaining why Sir Greyson and I felt
justified in our actions." He took a sip of his whiskey.

"Well, get on with it," the detective said.

"Sir Greyson and I approached Lloyd in the hope
that we could convince him to assist us in preventing
the colonel's manuscript from ever making it into the
hands of the Germans," Birdwhistle said.

"Why, the nerve," Colonel Livingston blustered.

Victor offered to refill the colonel's glass, which
settled him down.

"How exactly did you hope to accomplish this?"
Lord Browning asked.

"Well . . . we hoped by calling on his patriotism as
a British citizen we could convince him to . . . well, to
destroy the manuscript," Major Birdwhistle said.

"Why, the nerve." Colonel Livingston glared.

"I'm not proud of my actions, but we were desperate," Sir Greyson said.

"And? Did he agree?" D.I. Covington asked.

"No," Major Birdwhistle said.

"What happened?" D.I. Covington said.

After a long pause, Sir Greyson muttered, "He
laughed at us."

"Ha!" Colonel Livingston bellowed. "Wouldn't give
in to your unlawful demands, so you killed him."

The room erupted in chaos as both Major Birdwhistle and Sir Greyson fiercely denied having anything to do with murdering Sebastian Lloyd.

It took D.I. Covington several moments to regain
order. Eventually, the MPs calmed down.

"We did *not* kill him or anyone," Birdwhistle said.

"We even stooped as low as to offer him money. We offered to pay him five thousand pounds, but he refused. I never thought I'd see the day that I would resort to paying a dirty . . . traitor." Sir Greyson pursed his lips.

"Love for this country is the only thing that could have induced me to stoop to such depths." Major Birdwhistle hung his head in shame.

"That's it. That's the extent of our interactions with Sebastian Lloyd. He laughed in our faces, and we had words, but I swear by all that I hold dear. He was alive when we left him," Sir Greyson said.

"Of course they would say that. They've been found out." Colonel Livingston fumed. "Arrest them. I demand that you arrest them for the murder of Sebastian Lloyd."

Chapter 33

"Working on the next *Murder at Wickfield Lodge*?"

"Olivia, you scared me."

"I'm sorry. I didn't mean to frighten you." Olivia Townsend took a few tentative steps into the room.

I patted my heart, which was racing. "It's okay, I was writing and miles away."

"Am I disturbing you?"

"No, not at all."

Olivia sat down on the seat across from me. "I wanted to apologize for the way I behaved yesterday. I shouldn't have—"

"It's perfectly okay. No need to apologize."

"Yes, there is. I was horrible to you. This past year has been positively terrible." She paused and looked up to the ceiling. "How did Queen Elizabeth say it, this 'is not a year on which I shall look back with undiluted pleasure . . . it has turned out to be an annus horribilis.'"

"Understandable."

"Regardless, that was not an excuse to take my frustration out on you. For that, I'm truly sorry."

Olivia Townsend definitely knows how to apologize. I need to remember that for Colonel Livingston.

"Apology accepted," I said in the hopes of moving to a more comfortable conversation. "Is the panel discussion over?"

"No, but I've heard enough of Judith Hunter to last a lifetime." She smiled and paused a few moments. "I noticed that detective was still roaming around. Surely, the case is wrapped up now that poor Nora Cooper is dead."

"I suppose so, but then he doesn't take me into his confidence. Perhaps he just wants to make absolutely certain that Judith Hunter is safe."

"Why surely, Nora's death ensures that."

I shrugged. Olivia was trying to make a point. I glanced at my laptop and realized I didn't have much time to get home and dress for the banquet. I hoped she would get to the point.

"Paul and I were shocked when we woke up to the news that Nora tried to kill Judith again."

"You didn't hear about the death last night?" I asked.

"No. We were both exhausted after yesterday's events and both went back to the hotel and fell asleep. Neither of us moved until this morning." Her gaze darted around the room.

Ah, so that's the point. She wants to make sure that I pass along her alibi to Detective Pitt.

"Well, I'm sure he will confirm where everyone was, just as a matter of procedure. He mentioned he had some loose ends he wanted to tie up," I said.

"Then, he'll know that Paul and I couldn't have had anything at all to do with it. I mean, how could we? Judith admitted to pushing her over the bluffs. I believe there were witnesses, too. Your grandmother and that older woman reporter."

Interesting. The fact that Nana Jo and Dorothy witnessed the event hasn't been released to the press. The only way Olivia Townsend could know is if she or her husband had been there.

"Well, I better go and get Paul so we can get ready for tonight. See you later." Olivia Townsend walked out.

I sat for a few moments. Judith Hunter had pushed Nora Cooper over the bluffs to her death. Nana Jo and Dorothy both witnessed it. Besides, Judith didn't deny it. So, what was Olivia Townsend doing walking around the bluffs in the middle of the night at the exact time when Nora Cooper and Judith Hunter were wrestling for their lives? How did she know where to be and when? Why was she there? And why was she so frightened?

Chapter 34

My phone rang and Frank's picture popped up.

"Hey, what time is the banquet?"

"The reception starts at six."

"I have a plumber here. I'll run home and grab my tux and then I'll be by to pick you up. We may be just a bit late for the reception, but we should definitely make it in time for dinner."

Frank was normally as calm as a summer breeze blowing across Lake Michigan. Today, he sounded harried.

"You don't have to go. I can go by myself or we can skip it."

"No, I want to go, really. It's just been a bit crazy here with the plumbing issues. I've been looking forward to spending the evening with you. We—"

Frank was interrupted when one of his employees dropped what sounded like every pot in the restaurant. He mumbled a few words that I'd rarely heard him say. "Sam, I'm sorry."

"It's okay. It sounds like you have a lot of things going on that need your immediate attention. Why don't we skip tonight."

Frank tried to protest, but I kept talking.

"Honestly, it's one of the busiest nights at the restaurant.

You need to be there. I'll be fine. I'll take Nana Jo as my plus-one. You can make it up to me later." I grinned. I knew he couldn't see my face, but he definitely heard it in my voice.

His response brought a wave of heat up my neck.

"If I had known that's how you made up for missing a date, I might have insisted you miss a lot more," I joked.

We chatted a bit longer until the noise in the kitchen grew louder.

"I'd better go. Sam, are you sure? I can run home and be—"

"I'm absolutely positive. There's no way I'm going out with you tonight. I intend to hold you to every word you said." I giggled.

"It'll be my pleasure." Frank chuckled.

Nana Jo walked in. "What's with the silly grin?"

"My plus-one just arrived. I'd better go."

I hung up with Frank. "Frank can't make it tonight, so I told him I was bringing you as my plus-one."

"I guess that means I won't need this." Nana Jo held up a ticket for the banquet.

"You bought a ticket? That's awesome, but why?" I asked.

"Something doesn't feel right. We decided it wouldn't hurt if we were all there to make sure no one else dropped dead at this shindig. Dorothy has a press pass, so she's covered. Irma convinced Professor Smith to come." Nana Jo rolled her eyes. "Ruby Mae was going to have her godson—or was it her third nephew twice removed? Whatever, she was going to get a ticket from one of them, but now she won't have to. I'll give my ticket to her."

I hugged my grandmother. "You're the best."

"I know." She patted my back. "Now, let's go get gussied up. We've got a murderer to catch."

Chapter 35

It didn't take long for me to get dressed this time around. Frank wasn't coming, so I didn't have anyone to impress. Nevertheless, it was a black-tie event. I may have only been the cheap substitute author, but I was also representing North Harbor and wanted to put my best foot forward.

When I found out I was going to the awards banquet, I went shopping for a fancy dress. I couldn't decide between two dresses. One was more expensive and looked it. The other wasn't quite as fancy, but it was on sale. Ultimately, I bought both dresses. Today, I was grateful that I did. I wore the fancy dress Thursday night. Tonight's dress wasn't nearly as fancy, but it was still appropriate for the event.

I picked up Dorothy and Ruby Mae from Shady Acres Retirement Village. I was surprised when Irma came out too. "I thought you and Professor Smith were going together?"

"I told Smithy I'd meet him there. But I won't need a ride home tonight," Irma said.

I didn't even need to turn my head to the passenger seat to know that Nana Jo was rolling her eyes.

I drove to MISU's campus and dropped the girls off at the door. I lucked out and found a parking space not very far away. By the time I arrived, they were all waiting near the entrance.

The awards banquet was being held in the same room where it had been held just two days ago. Hard to believe it had only been two days. I couldn't help but glance to the area where Clark Cunningham had died.

"Sam!" Nana Jo shook me. "We're going to need to keep our wits about us tonight. No daydreaming."

"Oh, there's Smithy. Yoo-hoo." Irma waved her hand and then sauntered over to Professor Smith, who looked completely out of place in a tweed suit with a bow tie.

Irma was wearing a red sequined minidress with six-inch red hooker heels. Despite being well into her seventies, Irma still had amazing legs.

Nana Jo leaned down and whispered, "Irma and Olivia Townsend both must get their shoes at the same place."

"I didn't realize you could find six-inch stilettos anymore. I wonder where they get them?" I said.

"Irma said she orders hers from Frederick's of Hollywood," Nana Jo said. "It's a wonder she doesn't fall over and break her neck."

I glanced around. The crowd wasn't as big as it was the last time.

"Let's hope history doesn't repeat itself."

I turned to find Scarlet MacDunkin behind me. "Scarlet, I didn't hear you come up."

"Wondering which one of us will bite the dust this time?" Scarlet sipped her champagne. She paused a moment and then smacked her lips. "I feel like it's a game of Russian roulette and I survived the first round."

"That was extremely poor taste, but I don't suppose I should expect anything else from you," Judith Hunter said.

Scarlet stopped a passing waiter and handed a glass of champagne to each of us. "Judith, darling, why don't you take round two."

Judith Hunter looked like she wanted nothing more than to toss that drink in Scarlet's face. Instead, she put the glass to her lips and tossed it back. After a few moments, she smiled at Scarlet. "I guess we're back at you, Scarlet."

"I think everyone here already knows my grandmother, Josephine Thomas, and Dorothy Clark. Can I introduce our good friend, Ruby Mae Stevenson." I turned to Ruby Mae. "Ruby Mae, this is Scarlet MacDunkin and Judith Hunter."

Ruby Mae shook hands with both women.

"You look familiar. Have we met before?" Judith asked.

Ruby Mae and Judith played a quick game of six degrees of separation, but it only took two. After Ruby Mae's husband abandoned her and their nine children in Chicago, she had supported herself and her children cleaning homes for Chicago's elite. Judith's grandfather, Alex Savage, had been one of Ruby Mae's clients. The two of them spent the next few minutes strolling down memory lane.

Paul West and Olivia Townsend strolled around the room. In an example of history repeating itself, Scarlet waved the couple over. For a few moments, it looked as though they wouldn't come. Nevertheless, they came over.

"Join the party. We've been reminiscing, and Judith and I have been taking our chances at tempting fate." She held up her champagne glass.

"That's not amusing, Scarlet," Olivia said.

Detective Pitt walked in, dressed in dark polyester pants that were at least two sizes too small and two inches too short.

He wore a white shirt and a wide tie that looked as though it might have been stylish in the 1970s.

"Holy cow," Dorothy said.

"The man looks like a mortician," Nana Jo mumbled.

Scarlet laughed and snorted champagne through her nose.

Detective Pitt looked around the room. When his gaze met mine, I forced a smile and beckoned for the detective to join us.

"Ladies and gentleman." Detective Pitt nodded to each of us.

"Detective Pitt, I can't believe you're still here. Don't tell me you haven't closed the case yet?" Scarlet asked.

Olivia Townsend's face grew pale, and her eyes darted around the room like a scared rabbit.

"Just a few loose ends to tie up." Detective Pitt rocked on the balls of his feet.

"Like what?" Scarlet asked. "I mean, as a crime fiction author, I find this whole thing fascinating."

Detective Pitt straightened his posture and stood up straighter. "Well, I can't share a lot. It's still an active investigation. However, I suppose it won't hurt to say that we're still confirming details around the last minutes of Miss Cooper's life."

"Oh, like why she called Judith to meet her on the bluffs in the middle of the night." Scarlet grinned and then turned to Judith. "Well, we can't ask Nora, but fortunately for us, Judith is here. Perhaps she can tell us. What do you say, Judith?"

Judith Hunter glared at Scarlet. "You're disgusting. Nora Cooper was a friend and now she's dead."

"Was she? Was she really a 'friend'?" Scarlet used air quotes to emphasize the word *friend*. "Even though she told anyone who would listen that you stole her manuscript? That's not what I would call a friend. Oh, but then that fits your personality perfectly, doesn't it?"

Judith narrowed her gaze. "I did not steal Nora's manuscript. And, if you continue repeating that lie, I'll sue you for
whatever you have left. Which, I understand, doesn't amount
to a hill of beans."

Scarlet was furious and her face flamed.

"Oh look, your face is turning scarlet, Scarlet," Judith said.

"Stop it. I can't stand all of this bickering." Olivia turned
to Paul. "Let's go."

"Oh no you don't." Scarlet turned to face Olivia. "You
don't get away that easily. You're in this all the way up to
your fake boobs. Don't pretend you're so superior. You
wanted Judith dead just as much as anyone."

"I don't know what you're talking about," Olivia whispered. "Paul, let's go."

Paul West stared from his wife to Scarlet to Judith.

"You know exactly what I'm talking about. You only
look like an airhead. You're not nearly as dumb as you try to
make yourself out to be." Scarlet took a sip of her drink for
courage. "You know that your husband is still having an affair
with Judith."

"That's not true," Olivia whispered.

Olivia glanced from Judith to Paul. "Tell her. Tell her it
isn't true."

Paul West ran his hand through his hair. "I've wanted to
tell you for weeks, but—"

"But what? But you couldn't find the right time? Well, here
we are. No time like the present to air our dirty laundry." Olivia
stopped a passing waiter and grabbed a glass of champagne.

Detective Pitt stared from one of the suspects to the other.

"Stop being so dramatic, Olivia. You're starting to sound
like Nora," Judith said.

Olivia screeched, "It should have been you! It should have
been you that went over that cliff." Olivia lunged at Judith.

Dorothy tackled her before she was able to get to Judith.
Overwrought, Olivia collapsed in a flood of tears.

Detective Pitt stared at the woman in shock.

I glanced around and saw that everyone was staring at the spectacle. "Perhaps we should take this somewhere more private."

Chapter 36

Paul West scooped up Olivia and carried her from the room. Dorothy escorted Judith Hunter while Nana Jo took Scarlet MacDunkin by the arm. Detective Pitt looked like a kid who's just been told there was no Santa Claus.

Irma rushed up to Ruby Mae and me as we were following the others out of the room. "I'm not going to miss all the fun."

In a nearby conference room, Olivia Townsend was curled up in the fetal position on the sofa, sobbing. Paul West paced from one end of the room to the other. Judith Hunter and Scarlet MacDunkin were glaring at each other from opposite ends of the room.

"Now, let's get the whole story," Detective Pitt said.

No one said a word.

"I don't suppose you want to hear the gory details of my affair with Paul," Judith Hunter said.

"I do." Irma raised a hand.

"Put your hand down," Nana Jo ordered.

I sat on the sofa next to Olivia Townsend and wrapped

my arms around her. "Perhaps Olivia can tell us why she lured Nora Cooper to her death."

"Olivia?" Scarlet said. "I thought it was Judith."

"Wait. Judith Hunter is the one that threw her over the bluff. Both of them saw her. Plus, she admitted to doing it . . ." Detective Pitt pointed from Dorothy to Nana Jo and then to Judith.

"Oh, Judith was the one who actually caused Nora's death, but she wasn't the one who called Nora." I turned to Judith.

"I didn't call her. I got a call saying to meet her on the bluff," Judith said.

I glanced down at Olivia. "You studied acting and used to be good at imitating voices. That was you, wasn't it?"

Olivia sobbed. "Yes. I called Judith. I disguised my voice and pretended to be Nora. I told her to meet me on the bluff to settle this manuscript thing once and for all."

"Then you called Nora and left a similar message for her?" I asked.

Olivia nodded. "Yes. I pretended to be Judith."

"But, why?" Detective Pitt said. "How did you know that they would get into a fight?"

"If I'm not mistaken, I think you planned to kill both of them. Am I right?" I asked.

"I had a gun. I planned to shoot Judith with the gun. I thought it would look like Nora did it. Then, I would push Nora over the bluff. I'd written a suicide note. Everyone thought Nora was crazy. She hated Judith. I wanted it to look like she was overwrought and killed Judith and then killed herself. I planned to leave the note nearby, but then she came." Olivia pointed to Dorothy. "I was afraid she would see me. So, I hid."

"Both Judith and Nora thought the other one had called." I turned to Judith.

"I didn't believe her when she said she hadn't called. I

called her a liar." She shivered. "We both said a lot of things. We got angrier and eventually things got violent. Nora lunged at me. We struggled and . . . well, you know what happened."

"But, why? I understand why you wanted to kill Judith. But, why kill Nora?" Scarlet asked Olivia.

"I had to. She saw me," Olivia said.

"She saw you do what?" Paul asked.

Olivia cringed and shrank back.

"She saw you put the poison in the champagne glass?" I asked.

Olivia nodded.

"Nora saw me. She saw me put the poison in Judith's glass."

"Wait. So, if you put the poison in the glass, you killed Clark Cunningham?" Detective Pitt asked.

"No. I put the poison in the champagne, but I didn't kill Clark," Olivia said.

"Now I'm confused, too," Nana Jo said.

"Nora saw you put the poison in the champagne glass?" I asked.

Olivia nodded.

"I put the poison in Judith's glass. I wanted her dead," Olivia said.

"You saw her, and you switched the glasses." I turned to Judith.

"You're as crazy as her," Judith said.

Olivia lurched up from the sofa and lunged for Judith's neck.

It took both me and Nana Jo to pull Olivia away.

Back on the sofa, Olivia wilted like a week-old flower.

"She's lying. Both of them are delusional," Judith said.

"Olivia isn't lying. She admitted that she put the poison in the glass," I said. "But Judith switched the glasses."

"You're crazy. Why would I kill Clark Cunningham? He

was my publicist. My friend. My former lover. I had no reason
to kill him."

"After the car accident, Clark Cunningham was in so much
pain, he got addicted to painkillers. He was a drug addict and
didn't remember much of anything. But he got clean. Then
Nora Cooper started reminding him about the manuscript. As his
mind became clearer, I suspect his memory came back clearer,
too. He might even have remembered some old files that would
prove that Nora Cooper actually wrote the manuscript."

Judith squirmed. "You're pretty good at fiction, but this
story is weak. The plot doesn't work. I'd say you need to go
back to the drawing board on this piece of fiction."

"I believe you found out that Clark Cunningham was
going to help Nora prove that she wrote *The Corpse Danced at
Midnight*."

Scarlet gasped. "You did steal it."

"Shut up! I didn't steal anything. I bought that manuscript
from Nora, fair and square."

"That's when he remembered about the manuscript—
Nora Cooper's manuscript."

"That was *my* manuscript!" Judith spat the words at me.

"I believe that Nora Cooper and Clark Cunningham cut a
deal. If he helped her prove that Judith stole her manuscript,
she probably even agreed to share some of her settlement
money with him," I said.

"Pure speculation," Judith said.

"Nora told us. That day in the green room. She told us
that she had proof that you stole her manuscript. You knew
Clark was the only one who could prove that you didn't write
that manuscript. When Nora Cooper said those words, you
knew you had to act," I said.

"So, I planned to kill Nora Cooper?" Judith said.

"No, not Nora, Clark Cunningham. That's when you
planned to kill Clark Cunningham."

Chapter 37

"You're nuts. I don't have to sit here and listen to this." Judith rose.

Dorothy and Nana Jo moved in front of Judith.

"You don't have to sit, but you're going to need to go through both of us to leave this room," Nana Jo said.

"Detective Pitt?" Judith said.

"Nobody's leaving this room until we get to the bottom of this." He pointed to Dorothy. "Stand guard."

Dorothy hobbled in front of the door and folded her arms.

Detective Pitt turned to me. "Go on."

"I don't think Judith planned to kill Nora Cooper. She knew Nora wasn't stable. Nora Cooper wasn't the threat. Nora had spent years in a mental institution. Judith told everyone that Nora was crazy. If the case ever did make it into a courtroom, no one would take Nora seriously. Who would believe flighty Nora Cooper was capable of writing such a brilliant book? Worst case scenario, Judith could pull out her documents proving that she paid Nora for the book. But that was a last resort. Clark Cunningham was there. People might believe him. They might believe that Judith had taken unfair advantage of Nora. That she had gotten her to sign the contract selling the manuscript while she was committed. No contract is legal if one of the parties isn't mentally competent."

"You're forgetting something. I didn't kill Clark. The poison was meant for me. That was my glass. Olivia already admitted that she put the poison in my glass," Judith said.

"Olivia did put something in your glass." I glanced over at Olivia Townsend.

"Nora saw me. She looked right at me. She must have been so focused on her hatred of Judith, that she blocked it out," Olivia said.

"Like she did with the manuscript?" I asked.

Olivia nodded. "Whenever she was stressed, she blocked out the details, but they always came back. I knew it was just a matter of time until she remembered what she'd seen me do."

Everyone turned to face Judith.

"So, Olivia put poison in my glass. She admitted it." She turned to Detective Pitt. "You need to lock her up. She's just as batty as Nora."

Detective Pitt turned to me. "She's right."

"Nora wasn't the only one who saw Olivia put the poison in Judith's glass. Judith saw it too. That's when Judith decided to make her move. She couldn't have known what Olivia put in the glass. She knew she put something in the glass, but for all she knew, it could have been a tranquilizer or a laxative. Judith couldn't take a chance that it wasn't deadly. That's when she added poison of her own and switched the glasses," I said.

"You're nuts," Judith said.

"Olivia, what poison did you put in Judith's glass?" I asked.

Olivia pulled a small bottle from her pocket and handed it to Detective Pitt.

The detective looked at the label. "Valium."

"Scarlet told us you used to work for a magician. That's how you learned some of the tricks of sleight of hand, isn't it?" I asked.

Olivia laughed. "I've gotten rusty. I used to be so good."

"Judith saw her chance. She put the poison in her own glass and then gave her glass to Clark," I said.

"Right. Clark spilled his drink and I gave him mine, but I did *not* put the poison in the glass. That was her." She pointed at Olivia. "She put the poison in my glass. I had no idea the poison was in the glass."

Detective Pitt walked close and whispered, "She's right. We'll never be able to prove she knew about the poison. We'll never be able to prove that she knew the glass was poisoned when she gave it to Clark Cunningham."

Judith smirked.

"But she told us. Remember when we were in the green room? Judith said, 'I wasn't the one who put the cyanide in Clark Cunningham's glass.'" I stared at Detective Pitt.

"Yeah, but I don't see—"

"That was one of the things you held back. You never released what type of poison it was. Olivia added valium, not cyanide. So, how did she know?" I asked.

The lightbulb finally came on. Detective Pitt turned and faced Judith Hunter. "That's right. Judith Hunter, I'm placing you under arrest for the murders of Clark Cunningham and Nora Cooper."

Chapter 38

Detective Pitt took Olivia Townsend and Judith Hunter into custody.

Paul West stared awkwardly at the door as Detective Pitt left with his wife and his lover. "I suppose I should go with them."

"That would be the humane thing to do," Nana Jo said.

Paul West hurried out the door, mumbling about missing out on the awards ceremony.

"Well, I'm glad that's over. I better get back to Smithy." Irma hurried out of the room.

Nana Jo looked at me, Dorothy, and Ruby Mae. "What do you say? Do we go out there and eat overpriced chicken?"

"I say we blow this joint," I said.

"Let's swing by the Gridiron and get a greasy burger and onion rings first. I'm starving," Ruby Mae said.

"Best idea I've heard all day," I said. "Dinner's on me."

"Chocolate shakes all around," Nana Jo said.

No one batted an eye at seeing four women in fancy dress eating burgers at the Gridiron. We did get a few odd looks

when Dawson and several members of the MISU Tigers football team spotted us and sat down to eat with us. Things got a
bit rowdy when one of the linebackers challenged Dorothy to
an arm-wrestling contest. And even rowdier when she won.
But, all in all, I had more fun than I'd had throughout the entire book festival.

I dropped Dorothy and Ruby Mae off at Shady Acres and
then headed home. Snickers and Oreo greeted Nana Jo and
me as though we'd been gone days rather than merely a few
hours. After letting them out to take care of business, we all
went upstairs.

Stuffed and wearing my favorite pjs, I sat down at my
laptop.

~~~

Wickfield Lodge, Drawing Room

Lady Elizabeth stared at the MPs. "After Lloyd refused to destroy the manuscript, is that when you
discovered that he was a German spy sent to recruit
Colonel Livingston?"

"What?" Colonel Livingston leapt from his seat,
but was immediately pushed back down by Detective
Inspector Covington. Lady Elizabeth's nephews, Lord
Victor Carlston and Lord James Browning, stood behind the colonel.

"That's ridiculous. I don't have to sit here and be
insulted." Colonel Livingston attempted to stand, but
was again forced back down.

"Perhaps Major Birdwhistle and Sir Greyson
should . . ." Lady Elizabeth inclined her head toward
the door.

"Gentlemen, would you please wait outside?" D.I. Covington moved toward the door.

The MPs looked confused and relieved as they hurried out of the room.

Once they were gone, all attention returned to Colonel Livingston.

"This is outrageous. I won't sit here and be insulted. I won't stand for it!" Colonel Livingston yelled.

"You can sit. Or you can stand, but you aren't leaving this room." Detective Covington turned to Lady Elizabeth.

"It's the only thing that makes sense." Lady Elizabeth turned to Lord Browning.

"How'd you figure it out so quickly? I just got a message from HQ." He pulled a telegram from his pocket.

"Blackmail?" Lady Elizabeth asked.

"How'd you know?" Lord Browning looked at the telegram. "Colonel Livingston had been paying large sums of money to Lloyd."

Colonel Livingston flopped back in his seat. "He was bleeding me dry. He saw my picture on the back of my book in a small bookstore at Cecil Court. He recognized me."

"You collaborated with the Germans during the last war?" Lady Elizabeth asked.

Colonel Livingston flinched. "I had no choice."

"You always have a choice," Lord William said.

Colonel Livingston closed his eyes. "I did it to survive. And I did survive. But then Lloyd found me. He demanded that I turn over the information that I knew to the Germans. He said if I didn't cooperate, he'd see that I was ruined." Colonel Livingston sat up.

"Don't you see? I would have been arrested and tried for treason. I would have been ruined."

Lady Elizabeth asked, "Is that why you killed him, Colonel?"

Colonel Livingston nodded.

"How? How'd you do it?" D.I. Covington asked. "How'd you get the poison in Lloyd's cup?"

Colonel Livingston smiled. "I put the poison in my own cup. Then I contrived an accident, and Lloyd dropped his tea. Then I merely handed him my own cup."

D.I. Covington grabbed Colonel Livingston. "Come along. You're under arrest."

"Victor, would you escort Colonel Livingston into the library and see that he stays there. I need a word with Detective Covington," Lord Browning said.

Lord Carlston hesitated a split second, but then nodded and escorted the colonel into the next room.

Once the colonel was out of the room, Lord Browning turned to the Scotland Yard detective. "I know you want to see Colonel Livingston put on trial for his crimes, but actually, MI5 has other plans for the colonel." Lord Browning passed the telegram over to Covington.

"But, he's a murderer. He's a traitor to the Crown and a bloody murderer," D.I. Covington argued.

"He is, but only the people in this room know that. If you arrest him, he'll go to jail and probably hang for his crimes," Lord Browning said.

"That's justice. That's what he deserves."

"But Sebastian Lloyd isn't the only German spy out there. If the Germans believe that Livingston is one of them, we can use him."

"Use him how?" Lady Elizabeth asked.

"We can use him to feed misinformation to the Germans. We have the manuscript. With a little finesse we can place just enough misinformation into the document that not even Colonel Livingston will know what's real and what's not." Lord Browning paced. "It's a way of deprogramming the enemy."

Detective Inspector Covington wasn't thrilled with the plan, but the telegram and a quick phone call to the chief inspector at Scotland Yard meant he didn't have much choice.

The fete wrapped up and Lady Elizabeth sat in the drawing room surrounded by her family, along with Reverend and Mrs. Baker.

"I can't believe they just let him go free," Lady Penelope said.

"Things are changing. Our nation is on the brink of war. I'm afraid things may never be quite the same again, dear." Lady Elizabeth stared at her niece. "We've been blessed. Our island nation has been isolated from the ugliness of the war and turmoil that has spread across Europe. But we can't sit back and watch evil roll unchecked across the land, destroying men, women, and children, simply because it's not our land."

Reverend Baker gazed into the fire. "I heard a minister, Reverend Charles Frederic Aked, speak years ago. He said something that always stuck with me. I may not be saying this exactly, but the heart of the speech was, '*The only thing necessary for the triumph of evil is for good men to do nothing.*' England can't sit back and do nothing. We can't allow evil to triumph."

Lady Elizabeth stared at the vicar. "I'm glad you encouraged us to have the fete. You were right. Our men will fight evil, and when they do, they'll remember days like today. They'll remember bright sunshine, green grass, and good people. It'll carry them through the war and bring them home again."

"May God bless them all, and may He bless this good land, this island nation. This England." Reverend Baker bowed his head.

I pressed SAVE and sat back in my seat. Detective Pitt called and told me that after a bit of prodding, Judith Hunter confessed. Without her confession, he wasn't sure he would have been able to make the case stick. Still, he wasn't sure what would happen to Olivia Townsend. I had no idea what would or should happen to Olivia Townsend.

Oreo and Snickers were curled up at my feet. In his sleep, Oreo gave a quick bark.

"Are you chasing squirrels?" I smiled.

I thought about my recently completed manuscript. It wasn't an epic that would change the world or save the Amur leopard. It was merely a fictional world where readers could escape. It didn't offer a solution for global warming. It offered a few hours of entertainment away from the troubles that plague our world. My book wouldn't save the planet, but perhaps it would create a chuckle. Or remind someone who is dealing with a difficult situation that at one point in our history, there were men and women who didn't stand by and do nothing when evil threatened their shores. They did something. They risked much, and they made a difference. And that was enough for me.

Acknowledgments

Thank you to my wonderful agent, Jessica Faust at Book-Ends Literary, my editor, John Scognamiglio, and all of the wonderful people at Kensington. Special thanks to Larissa and Michelle for allowing me to have a little fun. You two are the best!

Thanks to my freelance editor, Michael Dell, for being so flexible and for all of your help and the quick turnaround. You're the best. Thanks to my personal assistant, Kelly Fowler, for the support and promotion. You've given me the time I need to write and I appreciate all of your help and hard work. Thanks to Alexia Gordon for the medical advice. Also, thank you to Abby Vandiver and Debra H. Goldstein for the legal help. I truly appreciate all of the advice and especially for listening.

As always, none of this would be possible without the love, support, and encouragement of my family and friends.

Visit our website at
KensingtonBooks.com
to sign up for our newsletters, read
more from your favorite authors, see
books by series, view reading group
guides, and more!

Become a Part of Our
Between the Chapters Book Club
Community and Join the Conversation

Submit your book review for a chance to win exclusive
Between the Chapters swag you can't get anywhere else!
https://www.kensingtonbooks.com/pages/review/